CONTROLLING CIRCUMSTANCES

Jean Kelso

ISBN: 978-0-9951929-3-5
Cover by Chelsea Barnes

ACKNOWLEDGMENTS

Wow, where to start. For starters I want to say I hope you all enjoy this book as much as I enjoyed writing it. These characters mean a lot to me, some of you may recognize pieces of someone in the characters *wink wink*

I want to start by thanking you, my readers. Without you there would be no one to read my stories. So thank you for taking the time out of your day to read this book.

Thank you to my family and friends for always being by my side. I love you.

To my original beta team, you are amazing. Melissa, Shannon, Elizabeth, Tracey and Jessica. Your support and input means so much to me. I thank you for being by my side through the journey. To my new members who took the time to read through for the revised version, Amy, Pami, Jeannie and Rachael, thank you for taking the time to help out. I look forward to working with you on future projects.

To Casey Harvell. You are da bomb girl. Your business Fancy Pants Formatting is amazing! This girl rocked my original edits and my formatting. She helped me with so much, love you girl!

To Rachel Olsen at No Sweat Graphics. You rock my friend. Thank you so much for my original awesome cover.

Thank you Chelsea, Candice, and Brandi. You ladies rock.

Thank you, thank you, thank you! If I missed anyone. I apologize. I am not good at these. Now please read on, and remember to leave review.

PROLOGUE

Belle

I sit in a plush leather chair across from my doctor's desk where he sits with my test results. It's been a grueling time with test after test and pain pill after pain pill to ease the symptoms. Now I just need to get the answers. I look my doctor in the eye for those answers.

Taking a deep breath I speak bluntly. "Give it to me straight, doctor. You know that I understand the medical stuff, so don't mess around."

The doctor looks up from the folder on his desk with a grim expression on his face. "Belle, do you have anyone you want to call? Someone you want here for support?"

I bite my lip in uncertainty. With him questioning me, I know this isn't good. My doctor's really good, he knows what he's doing, but the man sucks at giving bad news. I roll my eyes and take a deep breath.

I reach across the desk and grab the folder. "No sir. There's no one, just me."

The doctor tries to stop me, but he isn't fast enough. I pull the folder in front of me and look down. It's here in black and white. It's plain as day. My jaw drops and I feel like I'm going to pass out. The last sound I hear before I do is the doctor calling my name.

CHAPTER 1

Belle

Today is Friday the thirteenth and surprise! Today's my birthday. I'm thirty years old. The big three-zero. It's supposed to be a happy day—you know, birthdays—and so far it isn't going so well. I'm not superstitious or anything, but to find out the news I never expected to hear in my lifetime on such a day...well, it makes a woman think twice. So yeah, Happy birthday to me! Isabelle Jones, that's me, but everyone calls me Belle for short.

I see cancer patients every day and they're usually older. I don't mean to stereotype—I know they can be young, too—but I never expected it to be me. I can barely wrap it around my well-educated brain that I'm thirty years old, still single, and now this. Well, I suppose I *did* put my career before men. Men weren't an important aspect of my life the past few years, especially after Mike—the man that ruined me in several ways. He took so much from me. He's the reason I've been so sealed off and afraid to live my life...to open up to anyone and be free again. To love myself for who I am or who I was. Eight years. The time sure has flown by, but no matter how much time has come to pass, the nightmares never end. Night after night, I can't escape them.

It's eleven thirty in the morning by the time I leave my doctor's building. I'm going to meet my best friend Mel for lunch to tell her my results. She's been so worried about me. We've been friends for eight years now. Meeting at university, both of us were taking the nursing course and have been inseparable ever since. It's like we're sisters or

2

something. She's the only person I've ever felt a connection to and could open up to, to tell my secrets. Mel had been there for me that unforgettable night and has never left my side.

"Well?" Mel reaches across the table and grabs my hand, staring at me openly, waiting.

I look straight into her bright hazel eyes, trying my hardest not to shed a tear, but one slowly leaks out and glides down my cheek. Quickly wiping it away, "It's cancer, Mel." I pause. "They found cancer on my right ovary. It hasn't spread anywhere. At least that's what the doctor said he's sure of." That's when the waterworks start. Tears begin to stream down my pale cheeks, unable to control them.

Tears start to trickle down Mel's face. She gets out of her chair and comes around the table to me before pulling me into a big hug. For a few minutes we just cry together. Everyone in the diner is staring, but that's okay. There's nothing wrong with two grown women crying together in public.

"We can beat this, you know." Mel sniffles in my ear then pulls back and looks at me. "What all did the doctor say? What do we do now?" she asks while she wipes at her nose with a napkin.

That's my Mel—the git er done girl. We talk for almost an hour as our tears turn to slight sobs then to gentle whispers between friends. We munch on some appetizers as I've lost my appetite to eat a full meal at this point. Mel now knows it all. The fact that the doctor said they had found the cancer early and should be able to get rid of it all, putting the cancer into remission. I still need to speak with an oncologist to discuss my choices of treatment to understand it all. It's not like I don't understand—I'm a nurse after all. I *did* take four years of university *and* received a degree. I *do* know a few things about the disease, but when it comes to your own health, you often freak out a little more than usual.

After our lengthy discussion, I feel a bit better. I little calmer, but still freaked out. I agree to meet Mel at the bar later as planned. She and some of our coworkers had planned a little gathering for my birthday, and I don't want to disappoint them no matter how upset I feel. Perhaps a distraction is just what I need.

I've done my best to push my news aside in my mind, now it's time to make myself feel better and go have fun for a night. I just have to find something to wear. I don't go out often, so my clothing selection is limited for the nightlife. Especially nightlife with Mel.

It's not like I'm your typical skinny girl or even your average sized girl. I'm a plus size woman, unfortunately. It's not that I haven't tried to lose the weight. I've done all the diets, all the silly, stereotypical fads. I even did the whole exercise thing, including yoga, but nothing helped. My body's determined to stay shaped the way it is. I never used to be on the plus side. I was your average sized girl at one point in my life. I was also a virgin once, but that was stolen from me. Since then my body has had a mind of its own. I live and deal with what I have and try to be happy, but if someone asked me to define happy, I don't think I could do it anymore.

In my closet I find a just-above-the-knee jet-black suede skirt, a burgundy, v-neck tight tank top, and my old thigh highs—what Mel calls "hooker boots."

I shower, straighten my just-below-the-shoulder length strawberry blonde hair, slip on some basic black matching lingerie and my outfit. I do my makeup to the best of my ability, making my eyes stand out the best I can with that smoky effect. I feel they are my best feature—being emerald green, it's best to make them stand out.

It's nine p.m. when I enter the large, modernized bar. Giant, multicolored lava lamps just inside the doors are lit up. Your typical "hot chick" coat check area is set up by the entrance, and the black marble tiled floors stand out in contrast to the flashy lights. A giant dance floor sits in the middle of the room, surrounded by several dark wooden tables and chairs. The bar isn't famous, but is always busy according to Mel.

It's early August, in which case I don't need a jacket. All I brought with me was a little black clutch to carry my wallet, cellphone and apartment keys. I take a deep breath and advance into the bar in search of Mel and my friends. I notice them over in the far corner. It's like Mel and I can read minds—she looks up at the same time I notice her. The look on her face—the look of surprise—makes me stop in my tracks.

I quickly check myself over. Just enough cleavage, check. Nothing on my shirt or skirt, check. Nothing dragging from my boots, check. So what is her problem?

I continue toward them with a weary look when Mel approaches.

"You look amazing," she says to me

I breathe out the breath I don't realize I'm holding. "You had me scared there for a moment. I thought something was wrong."

Mel smiles, "No, I just haven't seen you dress like this in so long. It's refreshing to see you, the old you, again."

I look down at my feet and feel the heat rising to my face. I know I blush a little as I look back up at her. "It's like you said to me earlier— *we* are going to beat this. So when you said *we*, I felt why not get all of *me* out to fight." I smile at her—the biggest smile I can manage to give and feel braver than I did moments ago. There's something about Mel that always brings the positive side of me out. I think it's her being such a positive person. She never lets anyone feel down on themselves. Being around Mel right now is what I need...and some alcohol wouldn't hurt either.

"You look great, too," I tell her, looking her up and down.

Mel has the body of a goddess. She's tall, thin and has great boobs. Her tanned and toned body blends well with her outfit tonight—just like it does every night and day. She has on a pair of tight blue skinny jeans, a hot pink halter top and her famous black with diamond studded cowboy boots. Her jet-black hair is wavy and pinned up on one side. Mel looks like the hottest cowgirl in town. We are complete opposites when it comes to clothing, but blend well. I can even smell the signature cranberry body spray she loves to wear. She's like me—not a big perfume person, but a body spray? Hell, yes!

I pull out a chair at the table and sit with the group of co-workers who are already deep into conversation, laughing and joking as if they have been friends their whole life.

It's later in the evening and I'm having a great time. The drinks are endless, the laughs are flowing and it's time for the music to start. The crowd's much larger than when we first arrived here—with not much space to move around. It's your typical dance bar for a Friday night.

I feel a tap on my shoulder and look over at Mel. "You see that good-looking bartender over there, he has been watching you all night," she says as she glances over to the bar with a smirk.

She must know who he is. Mel comes to this place often enough. She knows everyone that works here, probably. Mel's always talking about this place and the hot men that tended the bar. I'm sure she knows why he's looking, but she's not going to say anything to me about it. Mel's always trying to set me up, but I play along as usual. It isn't hard to do anyways—the alcohol's helping me relax and feel good.

"What?" I giggle.

I slowly turn my head toward the bar. At that moment I stare into the deepest, darkest blue eyes I've ever seen in my life. Butterflies turn in my stomach. I'm frozen in place and time—hypnotized by those eyes. I just can't look away. I'm unaware of the rest of my surroundings at that moment. It's as if everything else has melted away, with only him and I alone in the room. My heart rate increases and my breathing changes. How did this one man cause such a spark in me with only his eyes?"

CHAPTER 2

Belle

The moment is shattered. His attention is now taken by patrons at the bar shouting for drinks. The other bartenders snap their fingers in his direction and it doesn't help. *Reality returns to me, the music, the smell of alcohol, the people, everything.*

"Belle, you okay, hun?" I hear Mel ask. I turn myself back to the group, flush and sigh.

"OMG I feel great! Let's dance." Grabbing Mel's hand, I rush us out to the dance floor. Between my hormones from the instant lust I was feeling and the alcohol, the sky is the limit.

The music pumps and the beats are amazing, feelings them vibrate through me. Losing myself as my body moves with the music. I feel alive, I feel sexy—even if it's for only a moment, for this one night. I wish this night would never end because I feel free. There's no hurt, no pain, no history, my mind's blank and I love it.

After what seemed like staring into the soul of that gorgeous man, I feel like a new woman. I don't want to waste the precious time I have with that feeling. The possibilities seem endless.

"Wow, Belle, you're full of energy tonight. What's gotten into you?" Mel shouts against the music as we grind to the beat. "I need a break. I need to get a drink and relax now." She smiles and begins to leave the dance floor.

"Get me a drink? I'm going to freshen up and meet you at the table." I head toward the restroom. I bounce and bob my head to music along the way, feeling great.

Feeling refreshed, I leave the bathroom. I am about to turn toward the dance floor when I feel someone grab my wrist. Instantly, I'm on alert. Who would grab me in the middle of a bar?

I quickly think as they pull me into a dark corner and push me up against a wall. I let out a quick yelp as my pulse quickens, and suddenly feel an odd tingling sensation from the person's touch. *Fear? I don't know.* That's until I look up into those deep dark eyes I was staring into earlier this evening. I feel my heart stop for a moment, forgetting to breathe, fear all but forgotten. The tingling sensation zings to my core and causes me to want to squeeze my thighs together. *What the hell's going on?* I'm becoming unhinged.

I stare back into those eyes and try to speak, but stammering is what I get. "Wh... wh..." I just can't get the words out. Next thing I know, I feel warm, moist lips on mine, searching, invading my mouth. His tongue licks my lips and he tries to conquer my sealed mouth. His teeth nip at my bottom lip while his lips press on. It's as if he's asking for something, but do I want it?

I'm feeling rather buzzed from all the alcohol I've consumed. My mind's weak and I have no control over my hormones. Stupid hormones, they seem to be in overdrive right now. His lips feel so good on mine—So soft, warm and welcoming. His tongue—oh, his tongue—moist, reaching for mine and teasing. A heat starts to bubble deep in my loins. It's something I've never felt before. *What's this man doing to me?*

I surrender and open for him. Immediately, it's all tongue action. Then I feel a passion that I've only dreamed about and have never felt safe enough to open to. I feel his hand that was on my wrist begin to wander up and down my arm. He caresses me and the tingling sensation is indescribable. His other hand grabs my hip and he pulls me closer to him until we grind our pelvises together. I can feel his erection press against my pelvic bone, then against my core...my suddenly aching core. *OMG I think I am going to explode.* This feels so incredible, a feeling of such...of such...euphoria. He takes both my hands and raises them up above my head and holds them there while our mouths continue to explore. Its then my mind decides to take a detour, a sudden flashback moment, and I tense.

I'm back in his room—Mike's fraternity room. The night he stole what was rightfully mine. The night Mike thought that when I said no

I meant yes and getting help from his fraternity brothers was his right—a so-called fun thing to do.

We were in his room alone, Mike and I. I thought tonight would be the night. I was nervous. He had been waiting for me to give in and have sex, but I had been so afraid and was holding back. Mike had experience and I was a lonely, naive virgin. I'd heard stories about first times—the pain, the blood. When I finally agreed to try, I thought Mike would understand when I told him to stop, that I'd gotten scared. He knew my fears, but no, he got angry. He left the room and slammed the door. I couldn't believe he left me. I processed it quickly. Trying to run after him to tell him I was sorry, but when I opened the door, one of his frat buddies was standing there. He had an evil grin on his face. Then another frat buddy came to stand behind him. I backed into the room, beginning to freak out. Where was Mike? What was going on? Both of the men came into the room and not two minutes later so did Mike. Mike nodded his head at one of the men. I looked between them all and backed up against the bed with my heart starting to race.

"Mike, what is going on?" I asked him.

"I'm tired of you teasing me all the time. I want what's mine and you're going to give it…One way or the other." Mike smirked at me as he walked toward me and the bed. The other men slowly advanced as well.

"Please, don't do this. I'm sorry." Tears began to fall down my face. I'd never thought that Mike could be like this. He had been so sweet, innocent and kind.

Suddenly, I felt a jolt of pain and heat on my left cheek. Mike had just slapped me hard. Falling onto the bed. Everything from then on happened quickly, with my torn clothing and being pinned down, I had no time to process what Mike and the other frat boys had taken from me.

Breathing hard, I shake the memory. I'm not in that room right now. It's in the past, and this is the here and now. I push the handsome stranger away. "Stop." I look him in the eye and beg for him to stop.

He does stop and he steps back, but not far. He's in touching distance, but I needed a moment. Need to gather my thoughts.

I look down as I feel him take hold of my hands. It's an odd thing for him to do, but gives me a calming feeling all at the same time. I slowly gaze up his body and take a few deep breaths in the process. In that short time I can thoroughly check him out.

He looks about six feet tall, give or take, gorgeous light chocolate hair tousled about his head. Those dark blue eyes are now shining, full of concern. He has what looks like three-day-old scruff on his face. He's in need of a shave, but man it looks sexy on him. The whole outlook of the nose, mouth and chin just makes me want to melt inside. The look of a sexy bad boy, but I am unable to fully describe it.

He's hot and he kissed me into oblivion. He's not Mike. He's *nothing* like Mike. At least, I hope.

I quickly remove my hands from his. "It's just—I've never...I don't know you.... I...I...." I take a breath. "Oh—damn it, I'm stammering. I'm sorry." I blush at him and look down at my feet. I should be angry with him. He did force himself on me, but I sort of liked it. Not the whole restraining part, but the take charge part. Stranger or not, he didn't hurt me.

I feel his fingers on my chin as he lifts my head to look at him. "I'm sorry, too. I didn't mean to scare you."

Oddly, my body relaxes with that statement. "You didn't scare me, you just..." I think for a quick second. "Okay, yes, you did scare me, but not in a bad way." I give him a look that I hope he understands. My heart rate's steady—even with being in close proximity to this man. I want to kiss him again, but I still don't know his name. Of course, I'm not that forward.

"I understand," he speaks huskily. "A strange man groping you in a dark corner can do that. I'm sorry, but I needed to taste you." He looks down at me with hooded eyes and leans closer to me, our hips touching once again.

Suddenly, my hands are above my head and against the wall. The guy leans in and starts to nibble on my bottom lip, feeling his tongue and the gentle tug of teeth.

"My name's Gabe, and yes, I'm very happy to meet you, Belle," he whispers while slowly moving his playful nibbles down my chin and then to the side of my neck.

OMG, OMG, OMG. My mind screams at me. *I'm restrained. Don't freak out, try to relax. He knows my name. What's going on? I need to get away, run, run, run.* My mind flies a mile a minute. *This can't happen, not again. I will not let this happen. Never again.* I begin to struggle and pull my hands free from his grasp. He isn't holding me tight. I hadn't realized this, but I still feel trapped regardless. I push him away and run down the hall, out to the bar area, and find Mel.

"I got your drink, hun. What took so long?" Mel looks at me. I'm sure she sees the fear in my eyes. Mel looks towards the bathroom and back at me.

I can't take it. I can't stay here or I may freak the fuck out. As I walk to the table I tell her, "I have to go," a tear springs from my eye as I grab my clutch off the table and run out of the bar. I pull my cell out of my clutch and type a quick text to Mel to say I'm sorry and I'll talk to her tomorrow to explain. I hope I didn't ruin the evening.

CHAPTER 3

Belle

It's one a.m. in downtown Toronto. The streets are busy. Various people wander the sidewalks, going from bar to bar on a Friday night. I finally slow my pace from a run to a walk. I need to catch my breath, and I'm only three blocks from my apartment. Everything should be fine—I'm fine. Then I hear that voice right behind me. That sexy, husky voice from the bar. Gabe. "Hey..."

Before I know it, I feel a hand touch my shoulder and it stops me dead in my tracks. I take a deep breath in and out. I know exactly what I'll be looking into—his eyes. Those sexy blue eyes.

I turn and, of course, I'm right, but something's different. The eyes, they look hurt...confused. His whole look seems cautious.

I still manage to yell at him. "What!"

Then his hand leaves my body. *No... touch me. It's okay.* Damn, I'm so confused.

I stand and stare for a moment. I can't think of anything to say. The only thought that comes to mind, and the only words to slip past my lips are, "Why me?"

I don't know what he expects from me. Not once in my life have I been pursued by a man of his caliber. His looks alone are beyond my norm. I mean, he's gorgeous, and in my mind I'm fat and ugly.

"What do you mean?" Gabe asks.

I shift uncomfortably and glance around the busy street before I return my gaze to him. "I mean just that. Why me? I'm no one—nothing. You're gorgeous and can probably have anyone you want,

12

and you" –I lower my voice to a whisper of innocence— "kissed me." It isn't as if I didn't thoroughly enjoy it—I did—but it scared the shit out of me. I've never felt such a rush being touched like that.

Gabe blows out a breath as he steps closer to me. "You're beautiful to me."

I can't help but laugh. I don't mean to laugh so much, but I can't help myself. Nobody has ever right out told me I was beautiful. Not even Mike during the full three months we were together.

"Why are you laughing?" Gabe questions me. "Do you not see this when you look in the mirror?" He looks sadly at me and softly touches my forearm.

I flinch but don't move.

"No." I'm quick to respond. "This…" I move my hands up and down my voluptuous body, "is not beautiful." I huff.

"Why did you run from me?" Gabe asks me. "I want to understand. I want to know you. I need to know you."

He leans in closer to me and his actions appear clear, but I lean away. He's a persistent one as he continues to pursue me. He reaches up and cups his hands on my face before he leans in and gives me a quick peck on my lips.

I shiver.

He asks so much from me. *Damn it, why now? Oh, damn, his lips feel so warm.* I need to think straight and I'm drunk. *Stop this now.* My thoughts run rampant about my situation, about the man who stands before me. *Wow, alcohol does bad things to your mind. It's a good thing I don't drink often.*

"That's a whole load you don't need to know." I sigh. "You don't know me, and I definitely don't know you." I take a few more deep breaths. "Let's just say it has to do with a past I want to forget and can't, and a present that I need to deal with." *Wow, did I just say all that to a stranger.* I cringe inside. *Since when am I able to speak so openly? Damn you, alcohol.*

"Thank you. Again, I'm sorry." Gabe takes my hand in his and manages to persuade me to turn and start walking. "Where do you live? I should walk you home. I want to make sure you get home safe." A slow smile blooms on his face.

Jean Kelso

For some reason, I feel safe with him. I'm scared but feel safe at the same time. How confusing is that?

I allow him to walk me home and leave with him at my apartment door with no plans, no phone numbers. Nothing. I close the door behind me. Leaning against the door, I sink to the floor and begin to weep.

Go figure that I meet someone when my future is unknown.

CHAPTER 4

Belle

Ugh, Monday morning. Time for another day shift at the hospital. I had the weekend to grieve the results from the doctor and to unclutter my mind from the bar Friday night. I also took time to talk everything out with Mel. It's now a new day and time to start fresh.

I'm a few minutes early for my shift. I review the nightly report sheets to see what kind of day I'm in for. There were several traumas in the ER overnight and a few frequent fliers—as we call them—that have come in for medication refills. One case catches my attention and strikes my emotions strongly, almost bringing me to tears. A young girl, age ten with leukemia is being admitted to hospice. She's assigned to my workload until she transfers to the floor. I'm unsure if I'm going to be able to handle it. On any given day I wouldn't think twice about the case, but since my own health has taken a turn for the worse, my mindset is taking a turn, too. I know that it's unfair to my patients. It will be something I'll have to work around. I take a few deep breaths, grab the girl's chart, and review the orders.

After a few minutes, I go to the room where the patient is and the patient's parents greet me. I introduce myself and smile politely at them, then turn towards the little fragile girl—small and pale. Her stringy, light brown hair—which I imagine was once full and vibrant—lay limp on the pillow. Her big brown eyes look old and tired for her age, sensing they know that her time is almost up. Her cheeks are slightly sunken in. Through all of that, this young, brave girl still smiles at me. I feel the emotions to cry, but I pull myself together. I become the professional that I am and move towards the girl.

I do everything I can for the girl while she's under my care. I make her as comfortable as I can with medication, conversation and smiles. It's one of the hardest times I've had in a long time, but I make it through. I think the entire day on how the world can be so cruel, how such innocent people don't deserve to suffer such a horrible end. After talking with the little girl and her parents, I learn there's a point in time that you have to come to terms with it. You may not be happy about it—you're allowed to be angry—but there's peace at the end of the tunnel. You just have to deal with everything that comes, one day at a time, and remember that you're not alone.

After I transfer my patients that are being admitted to the floor to their rooms and discharge patients that are okay, I sit to have a quiet moment to myself. I have an email from my doctor saying that he set up an appointment with a female oncologist in the hospital that I work in for Wednesday afternoon. For now, I have to keep my head screwed on and get through the next two work days. Then I can find out my fate. It's going to be a very long two days.

Monday and Tuesday flew by so fast, but then again, I thought all my shifts went by fast. They're always busy with me running around my whole shift. I love my job though. It gives me satisfaction to know that I can help people when they need it the most. When Mel works a shift with me and we team up, the days are always wonderful. No matter what's thrown at us in the emergency room, we handle it together, and if it's in our hands, our patients will survive. Of course there are times when things are out of our hands, but we both have learned to thicken our skin and move on. Compassion is useful when necessary, but we can't break down every time a patient dies on us. If we did that, we wouldn't be nurses anymore.

With the past two days having flown by, Wednesday looms in front of me. It's time to face my fate.

The reality of it all sinks in as I try to contain my sobs while meeting with the doctor. I listen to my available options, and it makes it even harder. I understand every word, every medical term that comes from the oncologist's mouth, and yet I still can't believe this is happening to me.

16

CONTROLLING CIRCUMSTANCES

I'm able to hold my major breakdown in until I make it home. How am I going to do this? My parents and I don't get along at all. They always told me I was a mistake in one form or another, and their alcohol has always been more important to them than me. I have Mel, but she has her life to live. She can't be taking care of me all the time.

I take a deep breath, go to the liquor cupboard and pull out the tequila that Mel left a few months back. I start to pound back the shots, needing to feel numb, to feel nothing.

After about shot three I feel warm and tingly. I wander to my room and whip off my t-shirt. I start to strip out of my jeans in search of less restricting clothing when I hear a knock on my door.

"Who the hell...." I don't finish my sentence. I toss on a pair of yoga shorts and a skimpy tank top and run from my room. I chug back another shot of tequila because my priority right now is to be drunk, and then I proceed to answer the door.

Wow was that a mistake. I open the door to those eyes, that face, that oh-so-kissable mouth.

I lick my lips and lean into the door jamb. "Hi." I'm dumbstruck. I'm also three sheets to the wind. *Damn tequila.* All my inhibitions are gone and I *really* want to taste those lips again. I reach out to Gabe and grab the collar of his shirt, pulling him into me and kissing him.

What the hell am I doing? I don't know, and I don't really care. I feel buzzed, angry, lonely and seriously horny, especially with Gabe standing at my door. Nothing like this has happened before, and, I suppose, stupider things could happen. It has been told that alcohol does make you do stupid things. Also, it's been a long time since my itch has been scratched by a man, so what the hell? It's just one night. It's just sex, right?

I press my mouth to his. Gabe's body is close and my chest heaves with the lust that's within me. He wraps his arms around my waist and pulls me tight. I can feel his erection on my stomach. I can't believe I gave that to him. I slip my tongue in Gabe's mouth and he takes it willingly. It's like he wanted it all along. I hear Gabe growl as his hands glide down from my back to my ass. I moan loudly while still kissing him.

Gabe moves us into my apartment, kicks the door shut and shoves me up against the wall, never once releasing me in the process.

His body feels amazing against mine. He grinds his pelvis with mine as he dips his body level with me and hits my core with his rigid cock. A jolt of pleasure hits, and I moan again.

I can feel the heat rise from my core, up through my stomach, neck and into my face. I can feel the juices flowing inside my core. I'm so turned on—more so than I was at the bar. I feel Gabe's hands now on my hips, then they slide up my sides under my tank top and his fingers tease along the base of my bra.

I shiver at his touch, nipples hardening in the process. I start to breathe hard. I want more. I need more. I'm desperate for Gabe to give me the release my body aches for. Deep down I know I should stop. Underneath the alcohol and my stupidity, I know the man is a stranger. But he's a sexy stranger, and Gabe makes my body feel things it has never felt before. I want more of it, so I turn that part of my brain off and let go.

Gabe's lips are on the move and I love it. He nips my chin, around to my ear, down my throat, to the tops of my breasts. It all feels incredible and I let out a little shudder. Gabe's hands play at the base of my bra for a few moments before they move slowly down to my shorts. Goose bumps rise with his touch, my skin's sensitive to the touch of his fingers as they caress me.

"You feel so good," Gabe groans. His hands reach the seam to my shorts.

I gasp at his bluntness, his bravery to dare such intimacy, but I enjoy every minute of it.

Gabe slips one hand below the waistband, under my panties, until he finds my tuft of soft, curly hair. He swirls his fingers around for a quick moment and moves farther down into utter dampness. I begin to get lost in the sensual gift he is giving me, feeling the utmost pleasure.

Gabe groans. "So beautiful and so wet."

I'm in what feels like a fantasy-land. I can't think—all I can do is feel. His mouth, his fingers…everything. My skin tingles to his touch. A warm feeling swims through me. Tears of pleasure pool in my eyes. It's so much and not enough all at the same time, but it all feels so amazing. This man is driving me to orgasm and we haven't even had sex yet. I don't know what to do. I'm inexperienced, so I just go with what feels right.

I reach my hands up and run my fingers through Gabe's soft hair. I moan with every touch, every kiss. I don't want to push him away. I need to feel this, to feel wanted, to feel like a real woman—not a piece of used trash.

Gabe pulls me away from his body, noticing he is glancing around. Beginning to realize his motive as he pulls me in the direction of the couch. He pushes me down and crawls on top of me. His lips crush onto mine as he sucks my bottom lip, teasing it with his tongue and teeth. It's as if he is worshiping my lips and mouth. The sensation causes me to fall deeper into the moment.

Gabe begins to suckle my neck and nips my collar bone. I feel his hand glide down into my shorts once again. Surges of instant pleasure overtake me as his finger slides over the most sensitive portion—my clit. I can't help but notice how Gabe turns me on, how wet and excited he has me. Feeling as if I may combust at any moment, he slides his finger ever so slowly into me. I arch my body into it.

"Gabe," I mumble, putting my hands on his shoulders and digging my fingers in. His finger moves out and back in again in a steady rhythm as my body shivers, shudders, and my vagina walls clench tight around his finger.

Gabe must have felt this because his speed increases with his finger. A second finger enters as the rhythm continues. At this point I lose it, closing my eyes tightly, feeling as those fireworks are exploding within me. I can't contain my scream. "Oh my God!"

I feel the couch shift as I open my eyes to see Gabe moving from on top of me. I watch—happily dazed—as he quickly rips his shirt off, unzips his jeans, pulls them down and pushes them away.

I internally groan while watching Gabe strip down to absolutely nothing. The man has a hot body would be an understatement, memorized by his ripped abs, toned chest and muscular arms and shoulders complete Gabe. To complete the total hot body, even his cock memorizes me. Man, it's huge and hard. His body distracts me, and I don't realize what's happening. Before I know it, I can feel my shorts and panties being tugged off. I tense for a quick minute, closing my eyes tight and then open them again.

There's a dip on the couch cushion and Gabe's body rests over me once again. He pants as he brushes his hands up my smooth, supple body. He cups my large breasts and gives them a gentle squeeze. I moan. Moving quickly he reaches down for the seam of my tank top and pulls it up and over my head.

With my top gone, Gabe frees my breasts from the restricting material. Pausing for a moment, he gazes at my body before moving his head down to my exposed breast. Gabe takes a nipple into his mouth, sucking, teasing and nipping. Causing me to moan again in pleasure. He does the same to the other breast, then looks up at me with lust in his eyes. I return his gaze for a moment, and then squeeze my eyes shut. I can't believe this is happening, especially with a stranger, but I am loving every minute of it. I can regret it in the morning, but for now, I plan on living in the now, because it's possible I may not have a later.

It takes everything I have to keep my eyes open. Everything I feel exhilarates me. My chest heaves in and out with heavy breath as my eyes glisten from passion given to me from the man above me. Gabe seems to mirror my feelings, my breathing, and my thoughts. I can feel his hands still exploring my breasts, my abdomen—everywhere. I can feel his erection lying against my thigh, the tip wet with pre-cum as he waits for permission.

Yes! I scream in my head. Reaching for Gabe's erection and wrapping my hand around it, stroking it twice as I begin to guide it to my awaiting, swollen core, feeling it jerk in my hand. Once he's at my opening, Gabe stops, and I'm not sure why. I lean up into him with the questioning eyes.

Gabe looks down at me. He pants, his need obvious. "Are you sure?" he asks me. He looks like he really wants this, like he wants to devour every part of me.

I remove my hand from his erection and place it on his ass. I try to entice him forward, feeling his head at my entrance. I groan, "Yes."

That's all the assurance Gabe appears to need. Rolling his hips forward and thrusting into me, he leans into me and kisses me passionately again. My moans seem to encourage him further. He pulls back slowly and with more force, pushes forward again.

"Harder," I whisper and moan again with every sensation as he continues to move inside of me.

A few succulent kisses and two amazing thrusts, I explode under him once again. I arch my back and push my hips up to meet his. My legs wrap around Gabe's backside and I clench my insides around him. With both of my hands on his ass, I dig my nails in, continuing to explode. I quiver and shake as I feel the spasms of my vagina. "Oh, Gabe! Yes," I cry out.

With three quick, hard, deep thrusts, I feel Gabe's body tremble as he releases himself inside me.

"Belle....." Gabe yells out and collapses over my satisfied body.

I just lay there with him for a few minutes as we let our bodies settle from all the shaking and quaking.

Gabe pulls out of me and I whimper. He grabs the blanket resting on the back of the couch, pulls me close next to him, and wraps both of us in the blanket.

"Are you okay?" he asks.

Nothing like an orgasm or two to sober you up. The first I have ever had to be honest. I giggle and look towards him with a smile. "I feel amazing thanks to you." I bite my bottom lip while in thought. "I'm—ah, sorry for attacking you like that. I, uh—don't normally act like that. I blame the tequila." I laugh again. Then tears begin to stream down my face. I feel ashamed for what I just did. I'm not this person. I don't screw strangers to make myself feel better. *Damn tequila. Damn emotions.*

I can't believe I'm crying. Do I regret screwing him? No. Then what's my problem? Ugh. I lay there in his arms, curled up on my couch. I haven't scared him away, which is good, right? Trying my best to clear my emotions and take some deep breaths. He must have heard my subtle sobs as I then feel his hand on my head, stroking my hair softly. That feels nice—so nice I actually relax. My breathing slows, my tears stop. I close my eyes and fall asleep in my stranger's arms.

***

I wake suddenly to the nightmare I have often. I'm not in my bed so I look around the room and down my body. A man's arm lies across the swell of my hip.

I tense, realizing Gabe's still here. What am I doing? What am I going to say? I cried in front of him for a long time. My mind scrambles, trying to shimmy slowly out of his grasp. When I succeed, I stand beside the couch and look down on Gabe and his naked body. He looks peaceful and handsome. I re-cover him with the blanket and rush quietly into the bathroom.

After I shower and dress in a fresh pair of jeans and tank top, I return to the living room to find Gabe dressed. He sits on the couch. The blanket is folded next to him. When he smiles up at me my heart stops. *No, I don't regret this. No, I don't regret this.* I have to chant this to myself as I approach the couch and sit beside him.

"Hi," I whisper to him as if I were a shy little girl. I pick at invisible lint on my jeans as a distraction before looking up at him.

"Hi back. You okay?" Gabe smiles and reaches over for my hand. He takes hold and caresses his thumb over my knuckles.

"I'm sorry for crying," I say sheepishly.

"Nothing to apologize for. You had a moment, I accepted it. I'm here if you want to talk about it."

I can't believe my ears. This man—the man I just met who knows nothing about me—is sexy as hell *and* is willing to listen to my problems. Just the way he speaks makes me believe he means it, too.

"I'm not sure I'm ready. I just met you." I take a deep breath and look down at the floor.

I feel Gabe's fingers on my chin as he gestures for me to look up. Such as simple thing, a gentle touch. "It's okay. I'll be here when you're ready."

I feel as if I am going to melt. How can this man be real? How is it possible that he comes into my life now and makes me feel the way he does? It's madness. I need to think—I need time. Heck, I don't know what the fuck I need. I stand up from the couch abruptly. "Okay. Thank you, but I need to think. I'm sorry to kick you out, but you confuse me."

Gabe stands up, pulls me into a warm hug and whispers, "I understand." He releases me and instantly he's gone.

CHAPTER 5

Belle

The following Friday I see Gabe again. I haven't exactly been avoiding him, but I don't exactly know him *or* know where he lives *or* have his number. When Mel tries to convince me to go out again, I quickly agree. This time I wear a pair of my best fitting jeans, a copper-colored halter top, and my copper sandals. Wearing my hair up in a simple ponytail, but choose to wear a black choker chain around my neck, adding some meaning to the outfit and not seem too plain Jane. I was secretly hoping to see Gabe again, feeling the need to explain why I cried. If he wants anything to do with me, he needs to know what he's getting himself into. Since I was so forthcoming with my body, I should be forthcoming with my thoughts and feelings. Lay it all out and give Gabe the chance to run while he can.

The music is pumping as usual on a Friday night. The crowd's busy and Mel and I are both in great moods. The drinks go down smoothly and then Mel decides it's time for tequila. She waves the waitress over and orders two rounds of shots. When the shots arrive, it's not the waitress that brings them. A tickle of electricity crawls up my spine as I see the shots set down on the table.

That sexy, husky voice comes to life. "Ladies."

Gabe's right beside me and Mel has the biggest smile on her face. I blush. I didn't expect him to just show up like this.

"Hey, Gabe," Mel says. "Pretty busy tonight, eh?" She looks toward the dance floor.

"Yes, fairly busy," Gabe responds, but his eyes don't leave mine. His smile reaches his eyes. It's a flirtatious smile that I haven't seen before. "Are you ladies having a good evening?"

I try to get my voice back so I can speak. Mel looks at me and waits for just that. Finally, the words come become coherent. "Yes, thank you." My cheeks turn bright red and I smile. I feel like a teenager again—shy and blushing whenever he comes around.

Gabe smiles at us and saunters away.

I watch him walk away in awe, daydreaming.

"Belle! Earth to Belle!" Mel snaps her fingers in front of my face until I respond. In moments the shots go down the hatch. I never did tell Mel about my night with Gabe. I know I'm a horrible friend, but some things are just worth holding onto.

Its last call and I'm more than a little buzzed. Mel's completely trashed, so I escort her out to a cab and send her on her way.

"Do you need to be escorted home as well?" a voice asks.

I nearly jump out of my skin and turn to see where he is. I know that husky voice, but I didn't notice him standing there. Gabe leans against the outside wall of the bar beside a door.

"You scared the shit out of me, damn it." I strike a pose of annoyance before I relax. "Anyone ever tell you it's wrong to sneak up on people?" I huff.

"I wasn't sneaking. I was leaning here and then you were here. I saw the condition Mel was in and was concerned for your safety." A slight smirk crosses Gabe's face.

Oh, that was a good one, using my safety as an excuse.

Okay, since I *am* beyond buzzed, I have a hard time shutting up. "How do you know Mel? Did you sleep with her, too?"

The look Gabe gives me makes me jerk back. He looks angry. It leaves an uneasy feeling in me.

"No." He takes a sharp breath in. "Mel has been coming to this bar long before she ever brought you here." Gabe stands up straight and moves towards me.

"Stop right there." I'm very abrupt with my words. "Before you think of touching me, and I melt into your tantalizing touch. Fucking melt into you. First, we need to talk, damn it." I hold my hand up in protest and wobble as I try to hold my composure.

Gabe laughs. "You melt, do you?"

CONTROLLING CIRCUMSTANCES

I can feel his stare as it penetrates me. "Yes, now fuck off. Don't laugh at me." *Man, I need to calm down. I'm getting riled up for nothing.* "It's not everyday someone like you….." I look him up and down, lick my lips and continue. "Has any interest in a f'ugly like me." I huff loudly. "So we need to fucking talk."

"Did you just say f'ugly?" Gabe laughs again—a full belly laugh by the sound of it. "Is that even a word?" He's not laughing at me now. He actually looks serious.

"Yes f'ugly. Fat and ugly combined. F'ugly." I can't help but let out a low giggle myself. "Anyways, we need to talk, but I can't do it when I'm drunk." I stumble a little in my drunken state.

Gabe reaches out for me and prevents me from falling.

"Don't!" I mumble. I know he's trying to help, but my thoughts are a mess. If I don't walk away now, who knows what stupid thing I may say or do to this man--or with him--again? I situate myself and begin to walk home. Taking a glimpse over my shoulder I yell. "Tomorrow." I continue home without another backward glance.

***

Saturday morning, I feel a bit hung over. My head hurts slightly and my stomach is queasy. I get out of bed and dress comfortably in jean shorts and t-shirt, hoping a blast of caffeine will help and head to the kitchen to make some coffee.

After my second cup of coffee and some Ibuprofen I feel much better. Enough that I feel ready to go face Gabe.

I barely exit my building when I walk right into a well-chiseled body that smells super amazing, clean, fresh, and all male. I look up immediately and there he is. I step back and smile.

Gabe checks me over, smiles and takes my hand in his. "Come with me." I have no idea what he has planned or what's going to happen, so I allow him to lead the way. It feels nice to hold his hand, so who am I to complain.

We arrive at a small café on the corner down the street from my apartment. Gabe directs us in and towards a table. He even pulls out my chair for me. "Have a seat."

I do, even though I'm beginning to not really enjoy his subtle commands.

"You wanted to talk, so let's have it," Gabe speaks softly.

Right to the point—no simple pleasantries or anything. I'm a little nervous now. My foot begins to shake, tapping against the floor in a nervous gesture. Taking a deep breath I try to push aside the nervous me that is beginning to take over. I decide to pull up my big girl pants and begin.

"Well, for starters, what's your name?" I ask him bluntly.

"Gabe," he answers quickly.

"No, your full name." I won't let him get off that easily.

"Gabriel Mann."

"How old are you?"

"Thirty-three." Gabe smirks. A waitress approaches and he orders us both some coffee.

I chew on the inside my bottom lip and stare at the table while I think for a moment. Then I look up. "You said Mel was coming into the bar months before she brought me. So I guess…" I ponder how I ask without being rude. "How long have you been working there?" I search his eyes for any dishonesty in his coming answers.

"I don't work there as such. I own the bar, Belle."

The waitress brings our coffee. Gabe empties a creamer into his and takes a sip while he stares back at me. He pays no attention to the waitress who was ogling his assets before she walked away. Well, that's a good start, I guess.

Okay. Let me get this straight. He's hot as sin and owns the bar. He ignored the waitress who couldn't stop checking him out—I'm pretty sure if I was a man I wouldn't have ignored her. I don't know how to take this all in. He seems to be too much…not real.

"You own the bar…I guess that brings me back to my original question. Why me?" I sit up straight and wait with bated breath. I concentrate on his eyes and his full facial expression for any sign of a lie.

"You won't believe me," Gabe speaks flatly.

"Try me."

"Okay. Well…for starters, you *are* beautiful." Gabe puts his hand up to stop me from objecting. He knows me all too well already. "No, you listen. You wanted to know why, and I'm telling you. You *are* beautiful. You are confident, intelligent, independent and mysterious." He puts his hand down on the table and sits back.

I see no hint of a lie from him, but still I have a hard time believing it. "You're right, I don't believe you," I breathe out softly. "Did I not tell you I was fat and ugly last night? Between my looks and my weight, what about me is beautiful?" I bite my lip, another nervous habit of mine.

"To be perfectly honest, I prefer some meat on my woman. There's nothing sexy about skin and bones. A real woman has curves—and you have beautiful curves, Belle." He reaches for his coffee and takes a sip.

"Oh, okay…well, thank you for your honesty." I mirror him and sip my coffee. I accept his words, but I'm not sure I agree. Fair is fair, and since he gave me a piece of him, I should give him a piece of me. "Okay, my turn, I suppose." I blow out a quick breath and look Gabe in the eye. "What do you want to know?"

"Hmmm…" He smirks. "How about the same common courtesy?" He takes another sip of his coffee and sets it on the table.

I take a few deep breaths to clear my congested thoughts before I begin. "My name is Isabelle Jones, but I go by Belle. The night you kissed me in that dark corner was my thirtieth birthday, and I'm a nurse." Wow, that came out easier than I thought it would. Then I accidently blow the lid of the pot. "And I have cancer."

Gabe's eyebrows shoot up and he whistles softly. "Shit, cancer. Wow, I'm sorry. That really sucks."

I know everyone responds differently when told, but I had to get it out there on the playing field, toss it into the game. "Yes. I found out the same day as my birthday. Nice gift for me, eh?" I sit up in my chair and mimic his position again. I hope I didn't freak him out too much. I know he's probably going to run. No one wants a sick woman.

"I'm sorry." Gabe looks at me with sadness in his eyes. "If there's anything that I can do to help, please let me know." He leans forward and reaches for my hand that rests on the table.

I'm not going to cry…No, I *am* going to cry. Damn it! A small sob escapes my lips. "I don't know why I told you. I guess I needed to tell someone besides Mel," I lie. I know why, but he doesn't need to know. I reach for a napkin with my other hand and wipe up the escaped tears. "I go for surgery on Monday. Doctors say they caught it early and hope to remove it that way." I shake my head and hold in another sob. I really need to stop crying in front of this man. He's going to think I'm a frigging train wreck with all the tears I continue to shed.

I excuse myself to go to the bathroom. I need the time to calm my emotions before we continue our conversation. I really want to continue to talk with Gabe. I feel good when I'm around him. I don't understand it. Being around Gabe seems to fill that void within me.

Fifteen minutes is how long it takes me to calm myself after my episode. Returning to the table, I sit in the chair across from Gabe once again. He sits quietly and sips what now looks to be a refreshed cup of coffee.

"Are you alright?" Gabe asks as he tips his head and smiles.

"I'm better now, thank you." I smile back at him and sip at my own refreshed cup. "I'm sorry for crying so much. It has been so much to take in since I was told about the cancer. Then you entered my life and paid attention to me in a manner no one else ever has. It's been too much to handle all at once." I sink into my chair and eye the man before me. He's a mystery all on his own. Gabe takes a chance on me — a perfect stranger — or so I think. I may have to ask Mel and see if she has been dishing out information about me. He doesn't seem to be running too far too fast. You have to admit, it is strange that he's still here, listening to me talk and cry. Most men would hightail it by now. At least they had in the past. Oh well. For now I'll take what I can get and take it one day at a time.

"My intentions were never to make you cry. I know a little about you. Mel did spill the beans a little bit." Gabe grins. "I want to show you what you are worth."

Chills run up my spine. I'm worth something? According to Mike, I'm shit. I'm a fat tease that didn't put out when he wanted it so he took it. But I can't think about that right now. This man wants me...me and all my f'ugliness. I don't completely understand why, but I guess I'll have to find out. "I'm trying so hard not to cry again. I'm sorry. You must think I'm a total wreck." A laugh bubbles up from my chest. I can't contain it. I think I'm losing it.

I wipe at my eyes, not noticing Gabe get up. He stands beside me with his hand held out.

"Come on," he says.

Demanding again? Jeepers. What is with this man, and why do I keep jumping when he says so? Still, I put my hand in his and get up. Hand in hand we leave the café.

We walk until we reach the door to his place, which turns out to be the door that he leaned beside last night outside the bar. We stand there in silence until he speaks. "Trust me?"

I look deep into his eyes and see that glint that I've seen before. I can't stop myself from answering. "Yes."

Gabe opens the door and escorts me up to his home above the bar.

We enter a large foyer, remove our shoes and he guides me into the next room. It turns out to be the living room. The room is huge. It has dark cherry walls, a rustic hardwood floor, a large flat screen TV on the far wall, and black leather furniture. Gabe has a matching coffee table with end tables. The wood looks to be a dark cherry wood and the tops are made of glass.

Gabe escorts me to the couch. "Sit down," he announces.

I sit without a word, as my eyes wander the room in awe. Everything is beautiful. I never thought such beauty could sit above a bar.

Gabe sits beside me and grasps both my hands in his. "Well?"

"This is beautiful." My eyes still search the room with wonder until they land on Gabe. His beautiful dark blue eyes shine brightly at me as I smile at him. He lets go of my hand with one of his and I feel that hand moving up my thigh. He still gazes at me, taking my breath away.

I feel instant heat between my legs as his hand moves up more to almost cup my core. My heart skips a beat, making my mind think of Gabe and *only* him as I lean into him and press my moist lips to his. I reach and wrap my hands around his neck to pull Gabe into me. Not sure if this is where he's going with this, but with that look in his eyes, I simply can't resist.

"Mmm," I moan. His mouth is warm and inviting.

I feel Gabe move into me, getting closer to feel me. I let him take the control, not going to deny him. I let him tease my lips as he nibbles them to encourage me to open. I willingly let him enter and his tongue touches mine, massaging together as Gabe suckles, nibbles and teases some more. The man sure can kiss.

Feeling the need to have Gabe closer, I tug him into me. He concedes and straddles my lap cupping my face and taking the kiss even deeper. My mind begins to swim with pure lust.

I can't think straight. Gabe's lips are warm and inviting. His tongue tastes so sweet and his hands feel so powerful. He's in control, giving into him, and he takes it willingly, feeling every nerve ending I have on fire.

Gabe's mouth nibbles its way around to suck on my ear and letting a moan escape. My ears are sensitive and he hit the nail on the head with that move. I let my head fall back and close my eyes, taking in every touch of his lips and breath. My heart begins to race, my breathing accelerates. His touch quickly turns me on.

I reach my arms up and place them around Gabe's neck before I move them down his back and to his ass. I want to feel it all, every part of him. With the effects this man gives me, I can't seem to get close enough to him. How is it that he can do this to me? Turn me on, make me hotter than hot. A perfect stranger—a man I just met can do it with a simple touch? No man has ever made me feel like this—feel worthy and free. It's a damn shame, too, because it makes me feel *amazing*. Horny as hell, but amazing. Even though I feel this way, deeply-rooted in my mind are the thoughts of being unworthy—the feelings of ugliness try to bust up and defeat the happiness I feel. I should be able to just feel and go with the flow, not have to fight my own thoughts. Ugh.

I feel Gabe's hands caress and then squeeze my breasts. It pulls me out of my thoughts. I lean my head forward and moan at his touch. Seeing Gabe lick his lips causes mine to automatically react, and I lick my own. Moments later he's on me, squeezing my breasts again. Running his palm over my sensitive nipples, I shiver to his touch. I never knew that I could feel this good, even through clothing, but I suppose when you're as horny as I am, everything feels good.

Gabe moves his hands slowly down to the hem of my shirt and slides his hands underneath. He urges me to release my arms from his body and pauses his kiss long enough to tug the shirt up and over my head.

CONTROLLING CIRCUMSTANCES

He takes no time at all to dip his mouth into the valley between my breasts, beginning to suckle. He knows how to make a woman feel good—damn good. Pressing my chest up to his face giving him what he wants. I don't want to seem desperate, but fuck his mouth feels wonderful in all the right places.

He licks the tops of my breasts and nibbles on my nipples through my dark purple bra, making me moan. Gabe's mouth works its way up my chest, my neck, my chin, and a finally peck on my lips before he pulls back.

I breathe heavily as I stare at him.

"Fuck, you taste so good, like vanilla, but I need to slow down, Belle," Gabe pants out.

"Okay," I whisper to him as I try to get my breathing under control myself. I don't know what it is about this man, but he can work me up so fast, it's unbelievable…and just a little scary, too.

Gabe shifts himself off my lap and sits on the coffee table across from me.

I begin to calm down from the excitement and feel a chill run through me. It's then I remember I have no shirt on. I find it beside me on the couch, grab it and pull it back on. "I am sorry." I give Gabe a weak smile.

He scrunches his eyebrows. "What are you sorry for? You didn't do anything wrong. I was losing control." Gabe takes a few deep breathes. "I don't like losing control." He shakes his head and looks at me.

Gabe's eyes give away the fact that I fluster him. I'm flustered too, but I'm not about to tell him that. No man has wanted me like this before, the way Gabe wants me. No one has told me that I am beautiful or have made me feel the way Gabe does. I'm not going to ruin whatever this is before anything really happens.

"Maybe I should go," I look down and whisper. "I don't know if I should be doing this—feeling this. I don't know you well enough. You're too much…and I'm not enough…" I ramble on and on.

"Stop that." Gabe reaches with his hand and lifts my chin. We make eye contact. "If you want to go I'll understand, but please stop belittling yourself to me." His words are soft. "You're an amazing woman. You may not see that, but from what I see, you are." The corners of Gabe's mouth turn up into a full-blown smile.

That smile does wonders for me. Heat rushes up and makes me blush.

Staring into Gabe's eyes, I search and wonder what it is about him that makes me feel this way. I feel wanted, but I'm unsure about everything. All I have to go by is a glint in his eye and a tingle in my tummy. Go figure.

I still don't understand how he knows so much about me. I was brave once. I may as well hit him up with some more questions. "Can I ask you something?"

"Yes." Gabe looks at me with a smile.

"Why did you ask Mel my name?" I search his face for answers— for any hint. "I mean, when and why?"

"Can I plead the fifth?" Gabe smirks.

"I prefer you didn't."

He takes a deep breath and lets out a sigh, "Well, I'll give you this much for now, and I hope this will do. I saw you and Mel together at the coffee shop about three months ago. She started to frequent my bar more and more." Gabe glances down to the floor and back up again. His eyes glisten in the light. "I saw the pair of you walking by the bar one morning, and that same evening Mel came in. I suppose curiosity got the best of me and I asked her your name." Gabe lets out a slow breath.

Gabe has known my name that long? He's known of me for that long. He's seen me, but I've never seen him? The thoughts start to swirl in my head. For three months, this man has wanted to know me. *Me*, he wanted to know *me*. Holy shit. I need to get out of here. I'm nervous and anxious, but excited, too. I don't know how to feel about this…what to do with the information he just gave me. Ugh.

"I suppose that'll do for now, but I *do* want to know everything when you're ready, I guess." I push myself up from the couch and try not to show Gabe my confused emotions as I get ready to leave.

Gabe reaches for my wrist as I turn. "You're still leaving?"

"Yes, I think it's for the best right now." I show as little emotion as possible. "I have several things to do and think through before the surgery." At that moment I move to the stairs and head down.

CONTROLLING CIRCUMSTANCES

I hear him follow, but I don't look back. I can't handle this right now. With my fucked-up emotions about him and Monday coming up fast, I need space...time...a drink? Yes, a drink sounds good.

I can't let a man into my life now...can I? Even *if* I seem to have a special connection with him, it's just not possible right now. Plus, what's with this control thing he was talking about? If I let Gabe in, he would need to know about Mike and about restraining me. I have limits. Will Gabe understand?

CHAPTER 6

Belle

Monday morning comes and my nerves are sky-high. Mel stayed with me last night knowing what I was going to go through today. It is six a.m. and Mel is in the kitchen making herself a coffee when I come out of the bathroom. As I peered through the mirror, I looked horrible. My skin is pale, my eyes drawn in and blackened and I have that simple look of fear of the unknown peeking through my ever-revealing eyes. I didn't sleep well in the night. I'm a wreck. My surgery is today and I have no idea what they're going to find once they get inside. My oncologist is optimistic about my prognosis, but with my luck, one can never be sure.

"Well…are you ready for this, hun?" Mel sleepily asks me as she yawns.

"I don't think anyone is ever ready," I reply and arch my eyebrows with an expression of defeat. I go to my room, grab my already packed bag, return to the living room and plunk my butt on the couch. "Hmm," I sigh.

"What's up, buttercup?" Mel walks over and sits beside me. She leans in and sets her head on my shoulder. Mel looks up to my face and sees the tears that start to stream down my cheeks. "Oh, honey, everything will be okay." She speaks softly, but firmly, "You're going to kick cancer's ass. It won't even know what hit it!" Mel jerks her body around and pulls me into a big hug.

"I know," I tell her. "I'm just worried. I want to get through this." I sigh and look her in the eye. "Also, I'm just getting to know Gabe, and I really like him. There's a strange connection between us. I want to know him and I think we can be something. That is *if* I live through this." I sob and wipe at the tears that were already running down my face.

Mel chokes up, "Oh, honey. You'll get through this. As for Gabe, I don't think he's going anywhere. I'm pretty sure the feelings are mutual when it comes to him with you." Mel pulls me back in for another hug and I let her.

We arrive at the hospital an hour early because I need to preregister. I'm nervous as hell. Once I'm registered, they direct Mel to a waiting room. They take me back to be prepped in OR One.

Now it's a waiting game. I sit in a little waiting room of my own in a small hospital gown, my legs jittering up and down as I feel like I'm going to vomit. I hope they call my name soon.

***

Gabe

I'm home debating on whether to go to the hospital or not. Belle has her surgery today, and I want to be there for her. I don't want to interfere. I know Mel will probably be there but still want to be there for my woman.

Fuck. Did I just call Belle my woman? Damn right, I did. I plan to make her mine as soon as this surgery is over with. I know we don't really know each other, but that's the joy of the relationship—getting to know each other.

I finish my coffee and grab my keys, slip on my shoes and head out. I don't pray much, but I am today. I pray that Belle makes it through her surgery with no complications. She seems to have had enough happen in her life, she doesn't need any more problems.

Mel is reading a magazine when I find her sitting in the waiting room. She eyes me up and down. I just shake it off. I know there's nothing wrong with my outfit—usual outfit of blue jeans, a tee and my Doc Martens. Women tend to check me out every once in a while, but for Mel to do it—especially when she knows I'm into her friend—

just makes me want to curse at her. I don't, because I have a reason to be here—same reason Mel's here.

I narrow my eyes at her, walk over to the chair across from her and sit. "How is she?"

"I haven't heard anything yet. I'm still waiting. She's been in there for about an hour now." Mel sets the magazine on the table beside her and crosses her legs.

I look at her intently. I didn't think the surgery would be that long, but who am I to say anything—I'm no doctor. "What would be taking so lo..."

Mel stops me mid-sentence. "Relax, Gabe. It all depends on what they find." She shifts her legs out and rests her feet on the floor again. Mel looks just as nervous as I feel. This can't be good.

"So did you get a chance to talk a little over the weekend? You know, to get to know each other?" Mel asks with a smirk on her face.

I nod my head. "Yeah, we talked a little. I took her for coffee and showed her my apartment."

"Well that's a—" Mel begins.

There's a beep from the overhead, "CODE BLUE OR ONE, TRAUMA PLEASE RESPOND, CODE BLUE OR ONE TRAUMA PLEASE RESPOND."

Mel jumps right out of her chair and screams. "No!" She starts to run.

I have no idea what's going on, so I jump up and start running after Mel. Panic begins to set in as I run after her, attempting to yell at her. "What's going on?"

"Belle is in OR ONE!" I see Mel starting to cry as she runs to I-don't-know-where.

I finally catch up to Mel, grab ahold of her and hug her tightly. I have no idea what a Code Blue is, and it obviously isn't good, but I need to be strong right now. Strong for Belle and strong for Mel too, I guess. Mel shakes like a leaf in my arms.

"Shh, just try to relax. Belle is strong. She'll fight this. You told me this yourself." I guide her back to the waiting room and hope someone comes to give us answers.

Mel's frantic. No matter what I try to do to help her, she can't get the tears to stop. She still shakes and she's pale. Mel's sobs are out of control. All I can do is hold Mel and let her get it all out.

36

"She can't die," Mel squeaks out.

"Don't talk like that. She isn't going to die," I grit out. Hopefully not so rudely that Mel takes offense, but I am already having a hard enough time keeping my thoughts under control. To keep them in a clear state of mind when everything is hunky-dory is hard. But not when you have a chick bawling her eyes out in your arms, especially when she's crying about the woman you care about. I'm not ready to lose Belle, so there's no way in hell I can think anything like that.

It seems like hours before the doctor comes to the waiting room to talk to us. He pulls Mel outside and directs her to another room to deliver the news.

I'm strung tighter than a fucking snare drum now. Fear creeps up of the unknown. I can't just sit here anymore and begin to pace the hallway and wait for Mel. Hopefully, she'll have some answers for me and ease my mind.

"Please be okay, please be okay..." I mumble to myself. *Maybe this will help...then again, probably not.*

About twenty minutes later Mel comes out of the room and she looks a little better than she did when she went in. The doctor smiles at me briefly and walks away.

I rush over to her. "Well?" I'm frantic for answers and plead with my eyes. I search Mel's face for answers, but she isn't talking. Why isn't she talking?

Mel suggests we move to a corner in the hall before she speaks. Her face is flushed and her eyes are puffy, but she's stopped crying, so that's a good thing—I hope.

"She's okay," Mel starts. "She was under the anaesthetic longer than they expected and her heart couldn't handle it." She takes a deep breath and lets it out slowly. "They were able to revive her and stabilize her heart with some medications." Mel looks down to the floor and winces.

I see that wince, and I know something bad is about to be said. "What else, Mel? You're scaring me here."

Mel looks up at me again and continues. "Belle's tests showed she had cancer in her one ovary and they had said it was just the one." Mel's body trembles while she speaks. "But once they got inside, they found the cancer was much more advanced than what all the tests had shown. It had spread so rapidly." Tears start down Mel's face again. "There was nothing else they could do. They had to do a complete hysterectomy on her." Mel's sobs are out of control now.

Again I reach over and pull her into a hug. "But she's alive? Will she be okay?" I don't know what to say with all this womanly stuff— I just don't know. "Does she know about the hysterectomy?" I need a little more information. I don't understand what's so bad about the hysterectomy when Belle is alive and going to be okay.

Mel chokes back her tears and looks at me. "Um, she hasn't woken up yet." A few more breaths. "They are bringing her to the ICU and the doctor said we can meet her there. She said that Belle should wake shortly." More tears run down her cheeks.

I see Mel cry, and I know there's something I'm missing. I lean against the wall and clench my eyes shut. I understand this is hard, but damn the woman needs to spit the shit out already. I look to her and raise my eyebrows.

Mel must have gotten my hint because she suddenly blurts out, "She wanted kids, Gabe. Even with all the walls she has built around herself, the one thing she wanted in her life, she can no longer have."

Well, fuck me. I feel like a complete dick now. I didn't even think of that.

Kids.

Fuck.

CHAPTER 7

Belle

I open my eyes slowly and try to swallow and realize I have a tube in my mouth. There are lots of beeping sounds coming from a machine. I dart my eyes around the room to see what's going on, to see if anyone's there. I start to panic. Why am I intubated still? A tear streams down the side of my face. I feel someone squeeze my hand and then hear them call out to the nurses.

It's Mel's voice. "She's awake. Someone get the doctor." Mel leans over to me so I can see her. She must see the panic in my eyes. "Shh, it's okay. Try to breathe normally. When they get the tube out, the doctor will explain what is going on." Mel continues to hold my hand tightly. I can see the pain in her eyes. Something's wrong—very wrong. I hope the doctors get in here soon. They need to get this damn tube out and explain what the hell is going on.

It feels like hours, but it's really only minutes when the doctor comes in and removes the tube from my throat. Being extubated is a horrible feeling, but being able to breathe on your own and swallow is a very rewarding feeling to gain afterwards. Nurses flood the room and assessments are done. IV fluid bags are changed, pain meds are given. They do the normal post-op routine. When the doctor feels I'm stable enough, and with Mel by my side, she proceeds to explain my situation.

"Belle, I'm Dr. Clark. I'm the doctor on rounds in the ICU right now, but I'm fully aware of your situation. I can explain everything to you if you let me." The doctor stands patiently by my bedside and waits for my response.

My situation…What situation? It was supposed to be a simple in and out procedure. Panic begins to seep through the cracks. If not for Mel holding my hand to reassure me, I may lose it.

"Okay, please tell me." I'm beyond scared to hear what the doctor has to say, but I need to know.

Dr. Clark explains how the cancer was worse than expected and how it spread rapidly. It exceeded all margins and my oncologist had no other option but to give me a hysterectomy.

"A hysterectomy? As in I can't have children, that hysterectomy?" No. It can't be true. The one thing in life I have always wanted, I can no longer have. How cruel can this world be? I burst out into tears.

"I'm so very sorry, Belle," the doctor states and leaves the room.

Mel sits quietly and lets me cry. She understands what this means to me. I had a pretty good childhood considering the parents I had, but I was an only child. I had always wanted a brother or a sister, but my parents didn't want any more kids, so I had always wanted a big family of my own. I want a little, blonde-haired, green-eyed girl or a little brown-haired, blue-eyed boy or two of my own running around a nice big yard with a big play structure and sandbox, a tire swing hanging from a big oak tree. The whole family would sit on the back deck, barbequing, laughing, enjoying life together. I can picture it all…but now that dream's gone.

This is the ultimate pain, to hear this news. I hurt with the pain from the operation and now with this news, I don't know how long it will take for the pain to go away. As I've thought before, how cruel can this world be?

I look around the room at the tubes that remain in my body. The IV, the catheter, the morphine pump and back to Mel.

I ask just one question. I know she can't answer it, but I still have to ask. "Why me?" Tears run down the side of my face and I lay there in silence.

CONTROLLING CIRCUMSTANCES

***

It's been a week since my surgery and I finally get to go home. My incision is healing well on my abdomen and all the tubes are gone. I feel pretty good considering everything that's happened—you know, dying on the table and all. The doctor said that I need to have two sessions of chemo treatment, but after that I should be in the clear. They just want the treatment done as a preventative measure.

It's time to leave the hospital and move on with my life.

The hardest part to deal with now is the fact that I can't have kids. That'll be the hardest thing for me. Out of everything I have ever wanted—besides having a good man to love me for me—I've always wanted kids, but that is only one aspect of life, right? Well, at least that's what I keep trying to tell myself so I don't break down and cry yet again.

I know chemo will kick my ass, but I'll get through it. I'll have Mel by my side, and with the two of us together, anything's possible. Right?

Gabe came to visit after I told Mel it was okay for him to do so. He didn't overstep his welcome which I am glad for—not like I'd say if he did anyways. I wanted him there, needing him to help fill that void that now will forever haunt me. I know Gabe wanted to make sure I was okay and to show me he cared and it was sweet. When he showed up with flowers and a little teddy bear, I just about melted. The man sure knows how to fill a void.

***

Today is Wednesday. I'm feeling a little more myself and think maybe I should get out of the apartment. I now have Gabe's number, and since Mel's at work, I think maybe I could invite him to go for coffee. Now that I'm feeling better, maybe —just maybe—I can let him in. I still need to do my chemo treatments, but if I can show Gabe that I want him around maybe he'll be there for me, too. I need to be more comfortable around him and get to know him better so this will be a good start—I think. One day at a time. I need to stop hiding from life and start experiencing it. With Gabe I think I might be able to do just that, so I call him.

He picks up on first ring. "Hello?"

"Hi," I say quietly. I still feel shy when I talk to him, but sure hope that ends soon. "This is Belle. I was wondering if you wanted to go for coffee." I did it! I asked! I made the move. I feel lighter for some reason.

"Hey," he responds, "I'd love to, where do you want to meet?"

"How about the diner we met at before?" I speak a little more confidently.

"Sounds good. How's twenty minutes sound?"

I feel giddy inside. "See you then." I go to my closet in search of something to wear that won't inflict pain on my incision. I settle on a nice violet sundress and white strappy sandals. I put minimal makeup on and a clear lip gloss before I head out the door.

I arrive at the diner a few minutes early, but Gabe's already there. He sits and waits in a booth. I smile to myself and walk confidently towards him. Gabe looks up just as I approach. His eyes are bright and his smile wide.

"Please sit," he says, and authority laces his tone.

My smile fades as I sit down. I look at him sheepishly and ask, "Why do you order me around?"

Gabe seems taken aback by my question. "I don't mean to order you around, per se. I'm sorry if that bothers you. I—uh…how do I explain this." He pauses and scrunches his brow up as he contemplates something. "I like control."

"Control? As in you want to control *me*?" I ask him honestly and tip my head to the side a bit in curiosity.

"Yes." Gabe draws the word out. "But not in the way you think," he adds.

Okay, this is a little freaky. What does he mean, not the way I think? I don't think I can let him have control over me. Not with my past. I don't even think I have the strength to let that happen. Do I let him know about my past? Or do I cut and run now? Shit, and to think I just decided that I wanted to get to know him…to have him by my side. Oh, what do I do?

"Okay, I think I need to get something on the table before we can go any further." I bite my lip and try to breathe normally. I try not to show the fear I have inside of me at what I need to say.

42

CONTROLLING CIRCUMSTANCES

Gabe looks at me expectantly, so I figure I better get this out before I lose my nerve. "I was raped at university." His eyes shoot open with what I assume is shock. Gabe looks like he wants to say something, but I stop him. "No, listen. I need to get this out before I can't say it." I watch Gabe's face and wait to see that he understands.

After he nods, I continue. "I was dating this guy for almost three months. I was a virgin and I had heard a lot of horror stories about losing one's virginity. I know they're just stories, but I was young and naive. Plus, I was holding off until I felt comfortable about it." I take a slow, deep breath. "I thought that on that particular night I was ready and when we...." The tears start to slowly stream down my cheeks.

"Stop," Gabe whispers to me. He reaches over to me and tilts my chin up so our eyes meet.

I sob. My body begins to tremble a little. It hurts to bring up the past so much. "No, I need to tell you." I try to contain my tears and continue. "Well, he got mad when I stopped. He left the room and slammed the door. I went after him after a few minutes, but when I opened the door to the room, two of his frat brothers were standing there. They wouldn't let me out of the room. When I backed up into the room, they came in. Then so did my boyfriend and shut the door behind him." I compose myself and look down at the table for a minute. I take a few breaths. The memories become so fresh in my mind. I lose myself as I tell pieces of that night...

Mike jumps onto the bed to pin me down. "I've waited and waited. Tried to be the good boyfriend and be patient. I tried to be nice. Well, I'm done being nice, Isabelle. I'm getting what you've held back, and I'm getting it now."

Mike straddles my body with his and he's no lightweight. He proceeds to grab at my shirt and rip it off like it's a piece of paper. He starts to bark orders at his friends. I swing my arms and try to hit at them, but one by one they grab my arms. I try to kick, but the weight of Mike on my pelvis is too much. I try anyways. Next thing I know, I'm tied to the bed.

"Stop!" I scream over and over. I don't know when it starts, but there's loud music on in the room. It drowns me out. I doubt anyone can hear me.

I feel wet lips on mine. They're sloppy, forceful, overly eager and impatient to reach their goal. They travel down my chin to my throat and then to my breasts. I scream again. I can hear the other men laugh.

I look around the room. In what seemed like no time at all, both of the other men have stripped. They're naked and as they watch what happens they both stroke their penises as if what happens to me excites them.

I feel Mike's hand slide to my pants and then they're undone. I whimper and start to chant, hoping Mike will hear me and stop. "No, please. No, don't do this."

But he doesn't stop. Mike's mouth wanders farther down my torso. His hands grip my pants. He leans up long enough to pull them down and off.

"Oh, mother fucker. I've waited for so long for this," Mike moans and then leans back onto me.

I can't stop crying. I try to fight back, but my hands are tied so tight that it hurts every time I struggle to set them free.

I try once more to get him to stop. "Please, Mike, stop," I beg. He finally looks up at my tear-streaked face with hooded eyes and smiles.

"Oh, poor Isabelle. So innocent and sweet, but not for long." Mike's smile widens and he glances to his friends. "Grab her legs."

Both men stop what they're doing. When each of them grabs a leg, I scream. The next thing I feel is agony. Mike rams himself into me so hard that I see stars. It hurts so damn much I think I may seriously die. I pass out for a short while, but come to before it is over.

The pain never goes away.

All the while Mike grunts and groans while he slams into me harder. His friends jerk off on each side of me. I want to die. Just when I think it's never going to end, it does. The men on each side of me ejaculate on me. Mike drains himself inside of me as I die inside.

The memory fades. I look back up at a fairly angry man. I'm sure Gabe isn't mad at me, but still, I need to finish. "To make this a bit quicker for you…Mike—that was my boyfriend then—he slapped me hard enough to knock me down onto the bed. His friends tied my hands to the bed and held my legs while Mike raped me." I see Gabe clench his fists. He must think I don't notice because he seems to be trying to hide them. This definitely isn't the reaction I expected from him.

"Where's this Mike now?" Gabe spits between his teeth. He seems to seethe with anger.

He's really angry, but why I don't know…I was the one raped.

I get my emotions under control. I wipe the tears from my face and fight my body to relax. "Last known address is the state penn." I shrug. I don't know where else Gabe expects him to be. I have no other answer for him. That seems to calm Gabe a bit.

I have more to say. I'm not sure where this will take us, but I have to get it out. "I understand that you like control, but I'm not sure that I'm a woman that you'll be able to control. I had my control taken from me long ago and I've fought since to keep it." I eye Gabe carefully for his reaction. I hope I'm not ruining something before it starts.

Gabe gazes at me for a few minutes then reaches for my hand. I give it freely. He gently grazes his thumb over my knuckles in such a sweet gesture. "Well, for starters, thank you for telling me about your past." Gabe pauses and bites his lower lip. "Secondly, I could never *take* your control from you. I want you to feel comfortable enough with me to either share or give freely the control that you hold to me. Not in your everyday life. It'd only be in special places." Gabe watches me closely. "I like you, Belle. I want to know you, to be there for you. I want you to be able to come to me for anything. There's something there, I know it. I just can't describe this feeling, this pull I feel between us, but I do want to explore it. I hope you will be willing to let us do that."

Wow, did he just say all that to me? Control in special places? What the hell does that even mean? He still wants to explore this...whatever it is with me? The giddy school girl comes to life inside again.

I can feel my smile get bigger. My cheeks begin to flush. "I start chemo on Monday," I blurt out. I have no idea why, but I do. Maybe it's because I want him there now that he said he wants to try things with me.

"Then I'll be with you." Gabe grins.

CHAPTER 8

Belle

The following night I go to Gabe's place. He invited me over because he said he wants to cook for me. Gabe wants to dazzle me with his "skills," which makes me laugh because he literally said that. It intrigues me. I want to see these skills.

I arrive at six in the evening as requested. I dress for comfort—to avoid discomfort to my abdomen— wearing a simple sundress in light green to brighten my eyes and white slip-on flats. It's nothing overly exciting—just plain clothing for simple me.

Gabe meets me at the door and looks handsome as ever. Sporting a pair of loose fitting blue jeans, a tight fitting black t-shirt and is barefoot. *Gabe looks good enough to eat...Maybe I'll eat him for dessert. Down girl, down!*

"Perfect timing! I just put dinner on the table." Gabe smiles broadly at me. I notice a dimple on his left cheek. *Damn, it's so cute.*

Gabe escorts me up the stairs and into the dining area. He pulls a chair out for me and I sit down. "Thank you," I say with my own broad grin.

I look at the food spread about the table and am in shock to see to the extent he's gone to in showing me his "skills." "Wow, this looks delicious," I tell him.

Gabe sits in the chair across from me and looks up to meet my gaze. "So do you." He smirks.

That dimple shows again. *How is it that I never noticed that before?*

CONTROLLING CIRCUMSTANCES

I feel the heat on my cheeks. *I'm so blushing. Why do I feel like a teenager around this man? He seems to be able to pull something from deep inside of me out, something that hasn't been able to escape in so long. I feel young and free. I haven't felt that in so many years.*

We enjoy a full dinner of baked chicken, mashed potatoes and asparagus smothered in butter. Gabe even has fresh buns. Boy, he sure does have "skills" in the kitchen, because all the food was beyond delicious.

"Well, you out did yourself. That was amazing," I inform him after I wipe my lips with my napkin.

"I'm glad you enjoyed that." Gabe grins, stands and walks towards me. "Shall we?" He reaches for my hand and insists I stand and go with him to the living room area. Of course, I comply. I have never denied him before, so why should I know?

Gabe brings me to the couch and encourages me to sit. He goes over to the stereo and puts some music on low. It's nothing particular that he chooses, assuming he was only wanting background sound. Returning to the couch, he sits down beside me.

Gabe's expression is full of anxiety and concern. He opens his mouth to speak, but then closes it again. It seems he's afraid to say something to me. What is he afraid of? I look into his eyes, raise my eyebrows in question and wait.

Finally, he speaks. "I have something I want to show you, but I don't want you to freak out." He still seems unsure of himself, so he speaks faster. "I know it's early and we can't do… anything right now, but I just want you to get a feel for what I need to show you. I hope you can be open and honest with me about it." He looks at me anxiously.

I'm unsure if I want to see what he wants to show me, but I have to be fair with him. I'm curious. I know Gabe won't push me to do anything I don't want to do. He understands it's too early for sexual activity since my surgery. I never could understand why you have to wait for at least a month before intercourse—the surgery was in my abdomen, not my crotch. Yes, even being a nurse I can still be biased and have my moments. I know the medical aspects of the surgery, but still—what does it really hurt?

"Okay," I say hesitantly. "Show me."

Gabe takes my hand. We stand together and he guides me down the short hallway to the room at the end. Gabe slowly opens the door. The room's dark, but I move forward into the area. I can see very little from the light from the hallway. Gabe steps in and turns on the light. I can't help my gasp. My heart rate speeds up, my breathing becomes erratic and my palms begin to sweat. I don't know why I'm nervous— It's just a bedroom…but it's *his*.

I look around the room. In the far corner sitting kitty corner is a king-sized bed covered with what looks like black silk and very plush pillows. On the night stand is a simple lamp and hanging off the side of the stand hang a pair of leather handcuffs. I turn to face Gabe and he's expressionless. He watches me take it all in. I flush and step farther into the room as I continue to look around.

The walls are pretty sparse with no pictures hanging. A huge window with sheer black curtains sits to the right of the bed. The color scheme is nice—very manly, I suppose. To the left is a closet with its door's closed. Not wanting to impose, I continue to move around the fairly large room and take in the scent of the man that lives and breathes here. I don't understand why he wants to show me his room. The floor's bare hardwood and a dresser sits against the far wall. Something on top of the dresser catches my eye. I'm not sure what it is, but it's a tube of something. Again, I don't want to impose, but I think Gabe notices my interest in the dresser because he speaks before I can.

"Go ahead, take a look," Gabe coaxes me.

I slowly walk towards it, curious to what it is. "Oh my." The words slip from my mouth. A tube of lubrication and small box with a picture of a cock ring sits blatantly on the dresser for anyone to see.

I don't hear Gabe come up behind me, but he places his hands gently on my hips in an intimate fashion. I feel it so much that I get those silly butterflies in my stomach again. *How does this man affect me so?*

"Do you like what you see?" Gabe asks me as he looks over my shoulder at me and smiles. He opens the top left drawer of the dresser and inside I notice a couple different vibrators, another set of handcuffs and some things I can't even name.

I take a deep breath before I speak. "Well, between the handcuffs, the stuff on your dresser top and everything in the drawer…" I shiver.

I'm not sure if it's my nerves or excitement. "I don't know what to think, really."

Gabe steps back to allow movement for me. The man seems so open about his sexuality—even after I told him about my past. I need to know. "Is there a reason why you have all of this out on display?" I bite my lip and wait for an answer.

"I only displayed it for you, to be upfront and honest. I don't want to have any surprises in the future that would scare you off." Gabe looks a little nervous, but completely serious all at the same time.

I move out of his reach and pace the room. My hand moves to my mouth and I begin to chew on a nail, an old, nervous habit. He displayed it for me...he wanted no surprises...well, shit. Handcuffs and sex toys? That's a bit scary.

"Belle?" Gabe calls to me.

I stop my pacing to look to him. I don't know what I really feel. Angry. Scared. "What?" I blurt out loudly.

Gabe moves closer to me. My freaking out must be noticeable. He pulls me into his arms. "I'm not trying to scare you, Belle. Are you okay?" Gabe begins to rub my arms up and down gently.

"I'm sorry. I didn't mean to let you think that I was freaked, because I'm not."

I hear him take a deep breath and blow it out. "Oh, thank God. I want you to be honest with me as I will be honest with you. I needed to show you this so you could try and understand the controlling part of me. This..." Gabe waves around the room and points toward the dresser. "This is where I like control, in here, the bedroom," he whispers in my ear.

I tip my head and turn to look at him. "I'll be honest with you, Gabe. I'm scared. Only because of my past, but I'm also curious. Does that make sense?" I question.

"It certainly does, babe." He winks and appears more at ease.

"Okay, hot stuff." I wink back and try to get back into a happier mood. "If I get a nickname, so do you." I laugh at the name I give him and then blush. I can't believe the stuff he showed me, but I suppose it makes sense. He likes control, and now he shows me toys. He likes to be boss in the bedroom. As much as that will be hard for me, I think I may be able to try for him.

Suddenly, sinful thoughts begin to rise in my mind. The things I could do to him if he let me. Tying him up, licking and kissing every part of his sexy body. The ideas are limitless. I'm not a complete idiot. I've seen movies and read books…but I suppose he's the one who wants control. He *did* say he could share it—or asked me to share mine, so maybe it'll be tit for tat. Only that'll mean that I'll have to let him tie me up, too. I guess when my body heals more…only time will tell. I look up at Gabe with a wicked grin. He'll never expect anything.

***

Gabe

After Belle leaves for the night, I lie in bed and think about her in my bedroom. How she looked at the lube and ring on my dresser top. When I opened the drawer, the color change in her skin said it all. I noticed the emotional turmoil she battled, but the glint in her eyes afterwards makes me hard when I think about the things I could do with her. Then the talk we had at the diner flashes to the forefront of my mind and crashes it all down.

If I want to be with Belle I may have to restrain my control and just see how things go. I know she's beginning to trust me. Just allowing me to show her my room and the display I laid out was enough proof to say she has some trust in me already, but I need to be careful. I'm not a dominant man. I enjoy some simple pleasures, and control of a beautiful woman just happens to be one of them.

The thought of blindfolding and tying Belle up sends a shiver down my spine. Her naked on my black silk sheets with her gorgeous reddish blonde hair fanned out on the pillow. Fuck!

My cock is hard as a rock. I reach down and squeeze it lightly. No! I shake my head. I'm in control. I close my eyes and take a deep breath. I need to plan out how I'll use my abilities to help Belle, to keep her trust and not scare her away.

CHAPTER 9

Belle

It's noon on Wednesday and I sit in the oncology ward. The curtains are drawn around me as my upper chest is revealed. The doctor puts in a central line that I'll use for my chemo. They give me some meds to make me drowsy and pain meds to help with the pain after the fact. The doctor explains everything about my adjuvant therapy treatment plan. My form of chemo isn't used often for the type of cancer I have, but since it's being used post-op and for preventative measures my oncologist felt this was the best route for me.

I understand it's going to suck. That's the gist of it. I don't look forward to the pain, the nausea, the fatigue and everything else that the doctor listed, but hell, if it prevents my cancer from returning or spreading, I'm game.

The central line is in and now I wait in a little boxed-in area for the nurse to come initiate treatment. Gabe went down to the café to get us both a drink, so I know he'll be back shortly. I reach for my purse on the side table and pull out the book I have with me to read. It's one that Mel suggested. She says it's good and juicy with lots of sex.

I make it through the prologue when both the nurse and Gabe slip in through the curtains. Gabe smiles and holds two coffees. He sits in the chair beside the bed I lay in. The nurse has a small bag of liquid in her hand which I assume is my treatment. She hooks it up to a machine and then hooks some tubing up to the line attached to me. The nurse mentions that my treatment will last about an hour and half and that she'll be around to check on me frequently. If I need anything before she makes it around, I have to buzz the call bell attached to the bed. After she dials in some numbers and explains about possible side effects, she leaves us alone.

"You okay, babe?"

I must space out a moment because Gabe's words startle me. I turn my head to him and smile. "I'm just nervous." I reach my hand out to Gabe. He takes it and gives it a gentle squeeze.

"I'm here. I won't let anything happen to you." Gabe returns the smile. He releases my hand, sits back in the chair and begins to drink his coffee.

I reach for my coffee that Gabe had set on the bed side table and take a sip. The doctor informed me not to drink too much liquid other than water for my first day since we didn't know how my body's going to respond. I brought a bottled water with me as it's listed on the sheet given to me prior to treatment of the dos and don'ts. The pills I had to take last night—to prevent a reaction to the chemo—has left me parched, so I'm very glad to have brought it with me.

Just having Gabe with me, I feel a bit better. I don't feel like talking, but I think Gabe knows this because he grabs a magazine off the side table, opens it and begins to read. His presence eases my mind. I set my coffee on the table and open my book again. If the rest of the book is as good as the prologue than I'm sure it will be amazing.

Fifteen minutes in my stomach begins to get upset. The nurse is in to check on me and when I tell her this, she mentions that this is normal. She opens the drawer to the table on her side and pulls out a basin for me to have access to in case I vomit. I get the water from my purse and begin to sip on that. Maybe the little bit of coffee I drank was too much. *No, the nurse told me it was normal, so I'll just let that thought go.*

Gabe looks up from his magazine with concern written all over his face. "Need me to get you anything?"

Even though I feel like I'm going to puke my guts out, I don't want him to be a slave to me. I just want him here. "I'm good. Thank you, though."

Gabe closes his magazine and sighs. "Belle, I'm here for you. Let me help you if you need the help?"

He stands from his chair, leans over me and kisses my forehead. "Okay, okay. I don't feel great, as you probably heard me mention to the nurse."

Gabe nods his head, turns his body from me and disappears through the curtains.

Where the hell is he going?

I'm glad the bed's set for me to be sitting up somewhat. I think if it was lying flat I'd feel worse. I stare at the curtain where Gabe just walked out because I'm curious to know what he's doing. *Did I upset him? I sure hope not. His support means the world to me.*

I just open my book again when Gabe comes back through the curtain with an ice pack and towel. I melt a little more. This man turns me to mush. I don't think I can stop myself from letting Gabe in. He seems to get sweeter and sweeter. He stops beside the bed.

"Tip your head forward, please."

I do as Gabe requests—maybe because he actually said please for once. Gabe sets the towel across my neck then lays the ice pack on top of it. He strokes his hand over my hair and sits back in his chair.

"The cool should help with the nausea." He grins.

I feel a tear leak from my eye. I wipe it and smile at him. "Thank you," I whisper. I look back down at my book and begin to read as I hear Gabe open the magazine he was reading earlier.

The hour and a half flies by fast. My nausea went away about fifteen minutes after Gabe placed the ice pack on me. The nurse checks on me every fifteen minutes and I remain stable.

Once they disconnect me from the medicine and cover my port cover—since it's fresh today I need to bandage it for a day or two—Gabe and I leave to go to my place.

Once home, Gabe makes me sit on my couch while he makes himself familiar with everything around. He brings me a glass of water and a couple Acetaminophen, since the nurse mentioned to watch for fever. Gabe sits beside me on the couch with his arm across the back and behind my head. Like I said, making himself familiar, comfortable.

Like I told myself before, I need to get comfortable with him, so I just go for it. I lean my body into his and tip my head to the crook of his underarm. I don't care if Gabe smells or not, I want to show my thanks. "Thank you for today." I look up at him and smile.

He leans down and kisses my forehead. "No problem."

Gabe reaches for the remote and turns the TV on with the volume down low. We sit snuggled on the couch for a while and fatigue takes over. My energy is low and I don't really want to move. I just want to rest my eyes for a few minutes. Maybe it'll help. Then I can get up and head to bed, but I know that won't happen. Being so close to Gabe feels too good. I take a long, deep breath and snuggle a little closer to him. My eyes close and I allow sleep to take over.

CHAPTER 10

Belle

Two weeks pass with little excitement. Here I sit for the last round of chemo since my doctor said only two sessions post-op. I'm happy that my doctor was right about one of the side effects. I haven't lost any of my hair. The drug he chose to use on me didn't have that effect. Don't get me wrong, if that was a side effect, I'd accept it, but with the vomiting and fatigue I've been experiencing, I don't think I want anything else. Now, treatment number two is today.

Gabe can't make it today—something about deliveries at the bar that he has to sign for—so Mel's with me. She freaks out a bit because she is so nervous for me. Worried about the effects of the chemo and such, so I send her to get us a both a drink while the nurses set everything up.

They hook me up and the medicine is running by the time Mel returns with a couple of bottled waters and a magazine. She smiles at me. Mel's skin is slightly pale as she takes in the setup, but I know she understands everything. She just hates the fact that I'm going through the whole ordeal. But hell, I'm alive, right?

We sit and chat for the full hour and half about work and just life in general. Mel tells me that there's a new intern at work that gets her panties in a twist and that she's thinking of asking him out. Of course I tell her to go for it.

By the time they disconnect me from the machines and we're ready to leave, I'm exhausted. I'm slowly learning that I've been taking advantage of my body for too long. Mel wheels me out by wheelchair to the car since the nurse in the unit doesn't approve of me walking out. She says I look too pale. I guess I look paler than I normally do, which is a first. I don't fight her on it. We nurses have been told that we make the worst patients, so I don't want to make things hard for anyone.

I'd told Gabe I would meet him at the bar for lunch after my treatment, but I'm not really up for any food. I have Mel drive me home so I can go to bed. I'm home ten minutes when my cell phone begins to ring.

When I reach over to the night stand by my bed and grab my cell, I see the name Gabe flash across the screen. I press answer and move the phone to my ear. "Hey, hot stuff," I say. My fatigue is loud and clear in my voice.

"Shit, Belle. You sound like hell. Are you okay?" His concern is more than noticeable.

I sigh and roll around in my bed. "Yeah, Gabe, I'm okay. I'm just exhausted. I feel like I was run over by a truck. This round of treatment was harsh." I yawn and lick my lips while I wait for him to speak.

"Well fuck, Belle. I should've gone with you. I should've delayed the delivery for another day," he grumbles.

Gabe sounds upset. I know he wants to be here for me, but he can't drop everything all the time. I know this and so should he. "I'm fine. I'm just going to get some sleep and I'll be good as new." I try to sound chipper for him, but being this tired, I'm sure he doesn't believe me.

I can hear Gabe's heavy breath through the phone. "I'll be there as soon as things are straight here," he growls. "Do you need anything?" he asks in a calmer tone.

I just want to sleep. Why can't he just give me that? I sigh again. What am I talking about? I've grown attached to this man. He's slowly been slipping into my heart and I haven't been able to stop it. "No, Gabe, I'm good. I'm going to sleep now. I'll see you when I wake," I tell him.

"Sleep well, babe."

I hit end on the phone and set it on the stand again. Then I roll back over and get comfortable. Sleep takes me not long after.

***

I wake to the sound of the television. Gabe must be here. Since I gave him that key, he definitely puts it to use. I slowly get out of bed and work my way towards the living room where I can see him. Gabe sits on the couch. Probably watching a movie.

I stop in the kitchen and notice my mail sitting on the counter. Another little piece of me melts for the man who sits not five feet from me. All the little things he does...He may not think I notice, but I do.

I lean down against the counter with elbows on the surface and my chin in my hands. As I stare at Gabe and smile, I take it all in. I never thought I'd let someone into my cold, broken heart. The past I suffered in college was so damaging, I never thought I'd be able to trust or love someone ever. Especially someone with such a strong character. Gabe snuck in. Little by little, he wiggled himself through the cracks I didn't think I had exposed, and my heart is beginning to accept him. At first my heart and mind didn't want to agree, but now with everything going on with my health, together they submit to him. Don't get me wrong, that little bit of fear is still there, but I'm able to box it off deep in the hidden depths of my mind. Thus far nothing has triggered it. I plan to have a heart to heart with Gabe when I feel better to discuss the future of us. That is, if he *wants* a future with me.

I pick up an envelope with a sigh and open it. I'm not prepared for what I find inside.

Dear Miss Jones,

I apologize in the delay of informing you about this piece of information, but your case with Mr. Stacks was reviewed. He was recommended for early parole and he was granted an early release. Mr. Stacks was released from prison last week. He was paroled with no controlled circumstances. Again, I apologize for the late notice.

Sincerely,

Robert Bonner

Attorney at Law

Jean Kelso

The letter slips from my hands and bile rushes up my throat, burning as it comes. I turn and run to the bathroom. I stumble into walls along the way and kick the door open. Then I fall to my knees and vomit into the toilet.

Memories of that night flash before my eyes and I vomit again. Chills creep up my spine, and I begin to cry. It feels like it just happened yesterday—the rape, court, everything. I squeeze my eyes shut and try to block it all out, but when I do that, Mike's threat starts to ring in my ears. *I will fucking kill you, bitch!* Over and over it repeats.

Gabe must have heard my urgent exit from the kitchen, because the next thing I know, he's pulling my hair from out of my face and holding it back while I lean over the toilet. I gasp in short breaths. While I retch bile, Gabe begins to rub my back.

"You okay, Belle?" Gabe's voice is full of concern.

I can't answer him. I don't think I can. My thoughts are a jumbled mess. They scatter about my past and the future I may never get to have. My whole body begins to ache as my muscles stiffen with every thought of the things Mike did to me back then. I can't remember if I told Gabe about him and what all he did to me. I think I did, but right now I'm not sure about anything. All I know is that Mike's out. He is on the loose. He is going to find me and he will kill me. He told me he would. For months after Mike was sentenced his friends harassed me with the same threat, but I could never prove anything.

I have to get out of here. I have to hide. I can't let Mike hurt me or Gabe. I lift my head and push up from the toilet, but I get to my feet too fast. Dizziness hits me quick and hard. I fall backwards into Gabe.

"Whoa, babe. Where's the fire?" He chuckles. Gabe holds me in his arms and stands us both up.

On my feet again, I don't hesitate. I shift from Gabe's hold, go to the sink, rinse my mouth and then brush my teeth. Once the feel and taste of vomit is gone from my mouth, I leave the bathroom. I head to the kitchen again with Gabe hot on my tail.

"Belle, what the fuck is going on?" Gabe asks. He sounds frustrated. I know he doesn't know why I'm acting this way, so I need to show him.

Once in the kitchen I grab the letter and shove it into Gabe's hands while I go in search of my cell phone. I need to call Mel. She needs to know Mike's out. She isn't safe either. Mel was in that

58

courtroom, too. She was on that witness stand on my behalf, helping me put that asshole away.

I'm in my bedroom already when I hear a very loud "Fuck!" come from the kitchen. Footsteps stomp down the hall.

"Belle, is this the asshole that hurt you?" he asks.

Yep, I must have told him. "Yes," I mumble as I begin to search the contacts on my phone. I don't look up at Gabe. I can't or I'll break. I need to control my emotions right now. I need to inform Mel, prepare and plan.

I hit dial once I find Mel on the list. She picks up on the first ring. "What's up girl?" she asks, always the chipper one.

"Mel." I get right to the point, no need to dance around it. "He's out."

I hear her gasp and I wait. As much as I know she is a happy-go-lucky kind of girl, when it comes to my past, Mel's a huge badass bitch. I know she's going to lose her ever-loving mind, so I count it off. Three, two, one...

"Motherfucking bitch! Are you serious?" I can hear her grit her teeth through the phone.

I want to laugh at her antics, because she sounds hilarious when she swears, but now isn't the time for laughter. "Dead fucking serious, Mel. He was released last week. Just got the notice today. Fucking lawyer sucks ass." I growl a little. The fact that my lawyer didn't prepare me for this makes me angry, but my fear overpowers everything. "What are we going to do?" I ask.

Gabe grabs the phone from my hand, glares at me and speaks sternly to Mel. "She'll call you back, Mel." Gabe hangs up on her.

"What the fuck, Gabe. I was talking to her." I narrow my eyes at him. I can't believe he did that.

"Belle! I'd like to be part of this. I *need* to be part of this. Let me in! Talk to me. Let me help." Gabe reaches his hand to the back of his neck and blows out a breath. "I know parts of the story, Belle, but not everything. Tell me everything, please." He sits on the bed.

I take a slow breath, exhale and sit beside him on the bed. I know it must be hard for him to sit on the sidelines and watch. I've never wanted to let anyone else in on my past. With it coming back to me...well, it makes it worse.

I can't let Gabe sit and stew over it. If he wants to help, then I'll try to let him. I face him and begin to explain my torrid tale. I tell every explicit detail—since he wants it all—from the beginning of when I met Mike in college, to how he treated me. I describe to Gabe every little detail of the night of the rape and the whole court fiasco. I explain that Mike was to spend ten years in prison, but according to the letter, he got early parole.

Gabe listens and holds my hands through the whole talk. I watch his facial expressions when I detail the rape to him. I think his stomach turns just as much as mine as I explain. It's not a night I want to live through again. It took a very long time to repress that memory and the triggers that came with it—and it all came back with that stupid letter. Eight years of a somewhat normal life now vanished. I hope I'm able to keep myself from shattering.

Gabe reaches up and pushes some loose hairs behind my ear. His touch is gentle and loving. I know the man cares. It breaks my heart to have to explain this crap to him, to drag him into my shitty past…but Gabe's touch feels nice. I'm beginning to crave it. I lean into his hand and smile.

Gabe looks into my eyes and leans closer to me. He takes hold of my face with his hands as he speaks. "You've become a huge part of my life, Belle. There's no way I'm going to let some asshole ruin what we have here."

I feel tears start to stream down my cheeks as I hear those words. Words I never thought I'd hear or deserve.

"We'll take one day at a time. If you need to stay at my place, then that's what we'll do. I'll keep you safe, Belle." Gabe leans right into me and presses his lips to mine. Passion takes hold of me, something that I've never felt before.

An emotion I can't explain begins to swim through me as our lips and tongues tango together. Fear be damned! Gabe's touch is a good distraction. I wrap my arms around his neck and pull myself even closer to him. Our bodies meld together as one, fitting like layers of skin--meant to be. I let myself go and let Gabe take over. His power over me, the control he has, is phenomenal. Gabe knows just what my body craves and gives it everything, sending me into utter bliss. All my worries and fears are forgotten—At least for the moment.

We're in each other's arms as we lay on the couch. Time to relax is a must. I'm rather tired after telling Gabe everything, and it feels good to just lay here in his arms. Music plays softly in the now dim room. Gabe runs his fingers up my torso and kisses my shoulder when I turn my head to look at him. "He's going to come after me," I whisper to him.

Never stopping his touch, Gabe wraps his leg around mine. "He can try, but he won't get to you." He leans down and kisses my lips softly. Then Gabe pulls me closer as if shielding my body with his. "You're mine to protect now. I'll do everything in my power to protect you, Belle. Now sleep." Gabe lays his head back down and I feel his muscles relax.

CHAPTER 11

Belle

A knock on my door startles me awake. I have to slowly wiggle out of Gabe's arms which still wrap around me. I cover myself in a blanket that's on the back of the couch and look at the time. It's midnight. *Who could be at my door at midnight?* A chill goes up my spine. Should I wake Gabe? No, I'm a grown woman. I can answer my own door.

I walk slowly and quietly to my door. I check my peephole and see nothing. A look back to check on Gabe which shows me that he's still asleep. I take a deep breath and slowly unlock the door. The door creaks slightly as I open it and I cringe. No one's outside the door. I peek my head out and look around. Still there's nothing.

"Hmm, that's strange," I mumble. I close and lock the door again thinking to myself that maybe I'm just hearing things, letting my situation get the best of me.

I make my way back over to Gabe, careful not to trip over anything in the dark. I bend over the side of the couch and kiss him on the lips. "Wake up, hot stuff. Let's go to the bed. It's cold out here." I watch Gabe stir awake and hear him grumble. Not much of a happy camper being woken up, I guess. I snicker to myself.

"What's up, babe?" Gabe yawns and grumbles. He blinks his eyes at me as he rolls to sit up on the side of the couch.

I smile at him and his nakedness. Gabe has such a strong, beautiful body. It's so hard not to touch him all the time, especially when he says that I'm his, which in turn makes him mine. "It's cold out here. Let's go snuggle under the blankets in bed." I start towards the bedroom.

Gabe isn't far behind, I know. I hear a low throaty growl, and I smirk. Then a smack on my ass makes me jump and giggle. I move faster, knowing what Gabe had in mind.

"Seeing that fine ass sway in front me…Damn the things you do to me." Gabe's on me in seconds. I don't get the chance to turn around or pull the blankets down. Facedown on the bed I go. I laugh as Gabe leans down with a smirk on his face. Another smack on my ass and my hands are over my head. Gabe's firm grip holds me and instantly my mind begins to wander.

"Stop!" I speak loudly. "Let go of my hands. Not this way, Gabe. I can't." I wiggle out of his grasp and turn my head to look at him. "Please…"

Gabe moves off of me and sits on the edge of the bed. He bends his head down to his hands. "Shit! I'm sorry, Belle." He looks up at me, a look of pain if I've ever seen it, and then back down.

I sit up beside him. I'm not mad at him—I just can't do it that way. Not yet at least. I still need to work on that. With Gabe's help, maybe one day soon I can. "Gabe, it's okay. I'm just not ready for that." I reach over and force him to look me in the eye. "I want to do that for you, but I need time." I plead to him with my eyes, my words— my heart. I'm falling hard. So hard for Gabe. I'd do anything for him, but I just need him to understand me first. Understand the triggers and help me get over them.

Gabe smiles a sad smile in return, but pulls me into him for a hug. "I got you, babe. Let's just sleep. Tomorrow's a new day. We'll start fresh."

We stand up. Gabe pulls the blankets down and tucks us both into the bed.

In Gabe's arms—with my head on his chest—I can hear his heartbeat, feel his breath and his warm skin against mine. I could sleep like this every night, but I know I have to take it one day at a time. I close my eyes and pray for a happy future with Gabe.

***

I wake from a restless sleep. Having had nightmares for the rest of the night, I feel exhausted. I need more coffee than my little Keurig can provide at one time. I stand in my sun-filled kitchen, wearing the tank and boxer shorts I tossed on prior to leaving my room. I lean on the counter and watch as the little machine brews the delicious smelling cup of caffeine. I figure if I watch it long enough that maybe it'll brew faster. Wishful thinking here.

I can hear Gabe in the bathroom. The water runs in the shower and I closed my eyes with a smile on my face. I can picture Gabe's naked body as water runs down his chest, his abs and sexy ass, and I get all tingly inside. *What's this man doing to me?* To think I once told myself that I'd never love a man, that I'd never deserve the love of a man. Here I am now. It's been a struggle, but I am actually happy. Who would've thought?

A knock on the door brings me out of my glorious daze. My coffee finishes brewing at the same time. I take my cup from the machine and walk to the door. When I look through the peephole I see nothing. I unlock the door and slowly open it. Again I peek my head out and look around. Nothing. "I must be losing it," I mumble to myself as I close the door and lock it again. I return to the kitchen to get a coffee started for Gabe.

The water pipes groan as the water turns off. I know Gabe's naked and wet. The thought makes me a little damp in the panties. I shake the thought of jumping him before I even finish my coffee. I leave the kitchen and head to the living room to sit in my comfy chair.

As I sip my hot beverage and soak up the delicious taste and smell of the French Vanilla roast, I almost don't hear Gabe come into the room. He holds my cell in his hand.

"Mel's on the phone, babe." Gabe smiles big and confidently. Only a towel covers him from the waist to his knees. What a glorious specimen Gabe is with his muscled-pecs and well-defined abs. I just want to eat him up. But I can't right now.

I return the smile and lick my lips. I try not to be too obvious as I thank him. "Thanks, babe." I take the phone from him and watch him walk back towards the bedroom. I assume to get dressed. "Hey, Mel. What's up chick?"

I can hear voices and traffic in the background. Mel must be on her way to work. "Hey, girl. Just checking in and making sure you are okay. I got a letter from the lawyer this morning about his release, too." I hear her sigh loudly. I know it scares her just like it does me. We were the only two witnesses to take the stand. We put him behind bars. Why wouldn't we be scared? "I think you and I need to have a talk soon. There's something else I need to talk to you about."

"I hope it is nothing serious. Are you okay?" It's not often that Mel openly tells me that we need to have a sit down. Since she wants to now, means something's up. "I'm free whenever you are. Just stop by when you can." I try to sound cheerful and brave, but I know she doesn't believe it.

"Just try to stay relaxed. I'll stop by after work. I'm working the short shift today. Love you chick." Mel hangs up.

I set my phone down on the table in front of me. Then I sit back and try to think of what Mel could have to talk to me about. *Is something going on at work? Did something happen between her and that guy she started seeing?* I wrack my brain and come up empty-handed. Guess I'll have to wait and see.

I hear Gabe before I feel him or see him. I'm not saying he's heavy, but in my small apartment, sound travels and it's a rather quiet morning. I turn just as I feel him touch my shoulders and lean down to kiss the top of my head.

"Mmm. Morning," I tease. "Coffee is ready for you in the kitchen." I look up at him and smile.

"So I need to go to the bar today for inventory. You want to come or do you have plans?" Gabe asks as he walks to the kitchen to grab his coffee.

I watch Gabe's gorgeous ass in his denim jeans as he walks. Sexual thoughts begin to swim through my mind. He distracts me so thoroughly that I don't hear him come back into the room.

"Belle, babe. Did you hear me?" Gabe chuckles.

I give an innocent smirk. "Nope." He knows exactly where my thoughts were. There's no way my thoughts aren't heating my pale skin to a nice rose pink color right this moment.

Gabe walks over to me and stands in front of the chair I sit in. He reaches down, takes hold of my hands and pulls me up. Wraps his arms around me, cups my ass and squeezes. "Is my girl thinking dirty thoughts after only one cup of coffee?" He grins at me.

I slide my tongue across my teeth and bite my bottom lip. "I'm not even finished my first cup." I pronounce the p with a pop and return his grin. I wrap my arms around Gabe's neck and stand on my tip-toes as I lean in for a kiss.

All I get is a little peck on the lips. Nothing to satisfy the craving I have for him at the moment. "You can't imagine how hard it is to say no to you right now, babe. But I need to get to work." Gabe squeezes my ass again and grinds his pelvis into me. I can feel his hardness and can't deny that he wants me. What a tease he's being! *Stupid men.* Never playing fair.

I take a slow, deep breath and stand down. I move my arms down to Gabe's chest and lean my forehead there as well. I want to be at least held by him. He moves his hands from my back side and cuddles me closer, into a tight hug.

"I understand, Gabe. Work first. Play later." I peek up at him and blink innocently. I'm not mad, just horny. But I can wait. I *will* wait. I have no choice.

"I'll make you all better later, babe. Don't you worry about that." Gabe leans down and takes my mouth in a deep, passionate kiss. With one more smack on my backside, Gabe leaves for the bar.

I finish my coffee and head to the bathroom for a nice cold shower to relieve the tingly feelings inside me.

I strip out of my tank top and boxers and lean into my shower. I turn the taps to start the water and test the water temperature with my hand while turning the power head on before I step into the refreshing spray and close the curtain.

The cool water does nothing to help the feelings that swim through me. The thought of Gabe in all his naked glory makes my body come alive. An ache between my legs needs my attention, and who am I to deny myself such thing. I start slow and caress my skin with the cool water. Up my torso, over my face, I drench my hair as I lean under the spray. I skim my fingers down to my sensitive breasts and trace circles around my nipples as they pucker to hard nubs. Goose bumps rise on my skin as my touch makes my nerve endings come alive. My breath increases as I move my hands down my stomach and glide my fingers across from pelvic bone to pelvic bone. The ache in me grows excessively. I shift my legs apart just enough to slide my hand between them and push my fingers into my damp folds. A moan slips as I hit a sensitive spot. It's a wondrous ticklish spot and it feels incredible.

I rub back and forth in my wetness and feel my arousal grow. I've never done this to myself, and now I feel like hitting myself for not. I apply some pressure to my swollen clit and it feels like my legs are going to buckle beneath me.

I hold my stance for as long as I can. The tingling sensation is strong and deep inside. I'm almost there. I reach up with my other hand and grab one breast. I begin to fondle a nipple. My breath grows deeper as my orgasm takes over. I see black and little white stars as my body shakes from head to toe. I have to lean against the wall to hold myself up until the aftershocks settle before I can finish my shower. I never knew pleasuring oneself could feel that way, so exhilarating.

After I finish washing my body and hair, I turn the water off and step out of the shower. I reach for a towel, wrap my body up and begin to dry off.

In my bedroom, I hang my towel on the hook on the back of my door and move to my dresser to pick out something to wear for the day. Slipping on a pair of panties and a bra—both in matching color of white. I figure since I'll just lounge at home for the day that I'll put on some yoga pants and a tank top. So with that decision, pants and tank of black and purple go on and I'm off to my kitchen to make another cup of coffee.

Walking into the living room I notice a breeze blowing the curtains around. *I don't remember leaving a window open.* I look around the room. Nothing's out of place.

"Gabe, you here, babe?" I shout out, but there's no response. As I move toward the window an eerie feeling comes over me. I shake it off and close the window. *I must have opened it, right?* I push the thought aside and go sit on my couch, picking up the remote from the table and flick the TV on. The girls at work have been raving about this movie *Divergent* since it came to theatres. Mel even brags about it and about the lead male character. I know I have to watch it. I may be thirty, but I'm not dead yet, right?

The movie just released to Pay-Per-View, so I one click to watch and see what the fuss is all about. Mel tells me that once I watch I'll be Team Four all the way. I guess I'll wait and see. I curl up on the couch with a blanket and my coffee and watch as the movie starts.

CHAPTER 12

Belle

Factions are picked and just as I get into the movie, my phone rings. Unknown number. With Gabe being at the bar, it's possible he's calling from the bar, so I answer.

"Hello?" Silence. "Hello?" I ask again. Heavy breathing is present, but no words. I look at the screen again to verify that the line didn't disconnect and put the phone back to my ear. I try again. "Gabe, is that you?"

"No," a voice growls in irritation. The breathing gets heavier and the hairs on the back of my neck rise.

"Wh... Who are you looking for?" I ask. Fear begins to dig at me as I speak. My number is private and not easily accessible to anyone. An unknown number and a growly voice don't mix well with me.

"You," the voice forces back.

My heart begins to race. The voice is creepy and mean, scary and unknown. I'm not going to listen anymore. I hang up and toss my phone back on the table. Then I jump from the cozy couch and run to the door. I make sure the door's locked. Things are starting to get really freaky around here. With the random call and the Knicky Knicky door knocking, I think I might just have to talk to Gabe about it, especially with Mike out of jail. Who knows what he might do?

I walk back to the couch and sit. Curling up with my blanket I look at the clock. It's still early so Mel won't be here for a while and there's no way I'm going to bug Gabe at work. I reach for the table and pick up my phone to set it beside me. *If anything else strange happens I just don't know what I'll do.* I take a few deep breaths and try to push it all aside. I'm letting fear control me and I can't let that happen again. Maybe I should call my therapist? *No. I can handle this.* This is petty compared to what I've been through. No need to bother him now. It's been years. *I can do this.* A few more deep breaths and I turn the movie back on. I need a distraction, and so far the movie— and of course the sexy Four—is doing just that. I settle back in and let my mind delve back into the life of factions and Mr. James.

Credits run down the TV screen and I'm still in Four heaven when my phone rings. My muscles tense and I slowly look down toward my phone. Gabe. I blow out a breath and pick up the phone. "Hey you," I speak softly.

"Belle, how're you doing?" His husky voice gets me every time. I take a slow, deep breath and blow it out. I know I have to tell Gabe about the call. There should be no secrets from him now that he knows about things.

"Not that great," I say.

"What's the matter? Did something happen?" Concern drips through Gabe's voice.

I bite my lip. This is hard to do. I know Gabe will get upset, but I have to tell him. "I'm not a hundred percent sure, but…" My breath quickens and I swallow the lump that I feel sitting in my throat. "I think Mike called me." I hold my breath for Gabe's response.

"Shit!" Gabe answers. I hear a clatter and then nothing.

A void of noise and Gabe's gone.

"Gabe? Babe, you there?" I ask as worry sets in. I knew he'd get upset. I dial his number, but the phone just rings. Over and over there's no answer. A lonely tear drop runs down my cheek. I reach up and swipe it away.

***

Gabe

When I hear the fear in Belle's voice, my chest aches. Somehow I know shit will hit the fan and fast. My woman needs me and there's no way I'm going to let her down. In an error of judgment, I hang up on Belle.

CONTROLLING CIRCUMSTANCES

I need to gather my control if I'm going to help her. I think back to all those months I stood by and just watched her.

Such a beautiful woman looking so lost in this massive world. She appeared alone in her thoughts as she walked by my place every day. After meeting Mel—who turned out to be her one and only best friend—my mind began to wonder about her. Why did this gorgeous creature only have one real friend in such a big place? She carried herself with confidence, but looked as if she were elsewhere while doing it. You could tell she wasn't out to impress anyone, but there was just a way about her that pulled my attention to her—a magnetism if you will.

I learned that Belle was a nurse in the ER at the hospital close by, and that she and Mel have been friends for many years. I wanted to approach Belle sooner rather than later, but believe it or not, my nerves held me back. Me, a strong independent man, allowing a silly thing like being nervous hold me back. Where was my control? Shit. I had to smash that down fast. I wasn't letting Belle slip through my fingers.

Her shiny light-red hair would blow in the breeze as she moved. Her hips swayed as she walked in her cute uniforms on her way to work. Belle would keep her head held high, but the grip on her purse was tight. Sometimes I'd notice her checking over her shoulders as if she was expecting that someone was following her. I began to tag her schedule and sometimes I'd follow her from a distance to the café where she'd meet up with Mel on occasion to grab a cappuccino. I learned from my so-called 'watching' skills that it was her drink of choice. Belle seemed to follow a routine of sorts. It intrigued me. I needed to know her.

After three months of watching, learning and beating myself from the nerves I'd never had before, I approached Mel and had a little chat with her. I convinced her to get Belle to come to my bar so I could see her in a different light. See if she would let her walls down at any time so I could strike and let my intentions be known.

Mel was a godsend to me and led me to my future. I think now how stupid I was for being so nervous about my beautiful girl. Had I known then what I do now, there's no way I'd change it. Belle's my woman and I'll protect her until my last dying breath.

***

Belle

I feel like a sack of shit. I sit on my couch, unable to get ahold of Gabe and unsure what he's doing. I must have spaced out. The next thing I know a loud bang on my door startles me and my body becomes tense again. I grip my phone for dear life as I curl my legs up and hold my knees to my chest. Fear is my enemy and I'm allowing it to take my life away from me.

"Belle! Belle, open up. It's me," Gabe yells through the locked door.

The sound of Gabe's voice makes every muscle in my body relax. I toss my phone on the couch and drop the blanket to the floor. Then I run to the door to let him in.

Once the door's open Gabe pulls me into a tight hug and begins to rub my back. "I have you."

He kisses the top of my head and moves us into my apartment, shutting the door behind us. We stand in the middle of the living room. Gabe lifts my head by my chin and looks me in the eyes. Compassion and empathy shine bright in his. He leans down and gives me a gentle but loving kiss on the lips before he leans back.

"Belle, I told you I wasn't going to let that bastard get to you." Gabe leans his head down again and presses his forehead to mine. "I protect what's mine, and I consider you mine." He brings his arms from around my back, down to my sides and then to my hands, which Gabe gives a slight squeeze. "Let's go pack you a bag and head to my place. I don't want you staying here right now. Not until that fucker is caught." Gabe stands there and just looks at me. He seems to wait for my approval.

"Okay. But I need to either call or leave a message at work for Mel. She was going to stop by when she was done her shift." I return Gabe's hand squeeze and let go.

In my bedroom, I begin to pack a bag of clothing and personal essentials that I'll need. I leave Gabe in the living room to wait. I need a moment to take in what exactly I'm about to do — and why I'm doing it.

CONTROLLING CIRCUMSTANCES

With my bag in hand, I return to the living room where Gabe stands and looks at my cell phone. I have a pass-code so I know he can't get into it. He looks so handsome as he stands there. Gabe takes my breath away every time I see him. To think he's mine. So he says.

"Having trouble?" I ask him.

Gabe turns and looks at me. "It's good that you have a code, Belle, but I'd never look at your stuff without asking." He smiles at me, but it isn't the full smile that I usually get from him. "Your phone beeped and I thought a message came through. Possibly from him. I was just going to bring it to you, but the screen turned on and asked for a code. It just shocked me, that is all."

I smile. I'm not hiding anything from him. Trust goes both ways and he should know that. "I have nothing to hide. Give it here." I move toward Gabe and reach for my phone. Once in my hands, I fiddle with the buttons and remove the code from it and hand it back. "There you go." I lean in and kiss his cheek. I don't know where all the fear I have has gone, but just being around Gabe I feel completely safe.

I watch as Gabe checks my callers list. He sees that the call was not the only 'unknown' number on the list. His eyes narrow and he looks at me. "He has called before?" Anger is evident in Gabe's voice.

I remember that call and having not gotten an answer when I answered. I can't be sure if it was Mike then or not...but then again I'm not sure it's him this time, either. "I honestly don't know. A few strange things have been happening around here." *Oops, that was a mistake. I wasn't going to tell Gabe about all that, but it's too late now.*

I hear Gabe growl deep in his throat. It's not a sexy growl, either. "Pardon me?"

"Nothing," I squeak out.

Gabe tucks the phone into his back pocket and faces me. "No, Belle. It's not nothing. Now tell me," he demands.

I don't want to upset Gabe further, so I explain to him about the door knocking and about the window. Gabe looks like he's ready to flip his lid. He immediately moves to where I set my bag and picks it up. "Get your purse and keys. We're going now." Gabe stands by the door and waits.

Jean Kelso

I put all my courage and faith in this man as I take one last look around my apartment. Then I grab my purse from the kitchen counter. Once I stand before Gabe, I hand him the keys, open the door and step out toward the next chapter in my fucked-up life.

CHAPTER 13

Belle

We arrive at Gabe's place ten minutes later. It's pretty handy that he doesn't live too far from me. I set my purse on the little table in the foyer, take my shoes off and walk into the living room. As I look around his place, it makes me remember the last time I was here and the room he showed me. Shivers run down my spine.

I feel Gabe before he speaks. His hand is on my waist as his breath heats my neck. "Are you okay?" Gabe's husky voice is gentle and full of worry.

I turn around in his arms and look up at him. Tears glisten in my eyes as my emotions begin to get the better of me. "I will be." I reach up and touch his face. After I hold him for a moment, I stand on my tip toes and press my damp lips to his. I want to show Gabe what I feel—minus the fear. I want to show him how thankful I am that he's here with me, standing up for me and helping me through a really tough time. Actually, several tough times. I don't know where I'd be without him.

I hear Gabe moan under his breath as he returns the kiss, but only briefly. He pulls back and takes my hands in his. "You can't let your emotions take over." He kisses me on the forehead and walks us over to the couch. "You sit. I will get you a glass of water." Then he disappears into the kitchen.

I sit on his cozy couch and look around. I take in what has become my life. Shit, I still need to call Mel. Things have escalated, and if Mike presses further, Mel could be in trouble, too. I turn my head as I hear footsteps. Gabe walks towards me with a tall glass of water with ice. I lick my lips, not realizing how dry they are. Gabe sets it on the table in front of me and sits beside me.

I look at Gabe and immediately tell him, "I need to call Mel."

With no hesitation Gabe reaches into the front of his jean pocket and pulls out his cell phone. He hands it to me with a grim expression on his face. "Use mine. I'll get you a new one. I have a buddy who I'm going to call to come and help out on your situation." Gabe moves one arm onto the back of the couch and around my shoulders. "Anything that leads to you…" He shakes his head. "I'm not taking any chances. You're getting a new phone with a new number and only the people who really need the number will have it. My buddy Jack is a computer whiz and I'm hoping he can track down the unknown number. Maybe we can locate that bastard before he tries anything else." Gabe pulls me closer to him and kisses me on the top of my head. All the sweet gestures he does. How can I not love this man?

I dial Mel's number on his phone and put it to my ear. It rings four times and then I get her voicemail. I know she's busy, so I just leave a message. "Mel, it's me Belle. Don't go to my place. Come to Gabe's above the bar. Mike found me. See you later and stay safe." I hang up the phone and handed it back to Gabe. "Thank you."

Gabe smiles at me with a glint in his eyes. "Anything for you." He moves into me and gives me a quick peck on the lips before he sits back on the couch. Gabe dials a number on his phone and puts it to his ear. "Hey, man. It's Gabe. Got trouble here. Need your help, man. My place, ASAP. See you soon." He hangs up, setting the phone on the table and looks at me. "Voicemail. It seems no one is answering their phones today." He grins.

I give Gabe a small smile and lean back into him. The warmth from Gabe's embrace gives me strength to talk. "So who's Jack?" I ask as I curl my legs beneath me.

Gabe runs his fingers through my hair and clears his throat. "Jack is a private investigator. We grew up together. Best buds is what we called ourselves." He chuckles. "Whenever one of us needs something, the other is there no matter what. Like brothers of sorts, I guess."

I can hear the steady rhythm of Gabe's heartbeat. His breathing is regular and relaxes me as his chest rises and falls. "Brothers. That's nice. I wish I had siblings. Mel is the closest thing to a sister for me."

Never once does Gabe stop caressing my head and hair. It relaxes me completely and I'm pretty sure he knows that. "Now don't get me wrong, we fought. Boy, did we fight. Not just verbally, either. We had the whole fists of fury going on at times." Gabe laughs. "But no matter what happened, we always had each other's backs. If someone bothered one of us, the other kicked their asses."

It's my turn to laugh a little. I tip my head up a bit to see Gabe's face and ask, "What were you like as a kid?"

"Well, to be honest, I had issues. I didn't have the lovey-dovey parents that most think. I was kind of wild and crazy at times and didn't have control of anything going on. It wasn't until I met Jack that things started to turn around for me. Oh, and that weekend I spent in jail helped a little, too." Gabe grimaces.

I sit up and look at him. I'm in shock. "Jail?" I squeak.

He just laughs. "Yeah, but it wasn't just me. Jack was there, too." Gabe shakes his head at the memory and smiles. "Jack thought it'd be fun while we were at his grandparent's cottage to go out in his new car with a baseball bat and play 'timber.'" Gabe sits back and folds his arms across his chest with a smirk on his face. He looks at me. "Did you know that it is illegal to smash peoples' mail boxes with a baseball bat as you drive by them?"

I can't contain the smirk that rises to my mouth. A laugh bubbles out. This man's taking my heart and making it his. It amazes me to hear that story and to see him now as the man he's become. The lessons he must've learned. I shake my head at him. "You were crazy."

Gabe fakes being hurt. "Hey, what were two sixteen year old boys to do on a weekend when bored? Especially being out in the country?" Then Gabe laughs and pulls me in for a hug.

We talk about our childhoods for what seems like hours. Never once do we lose contact with each other, always touching in some way. There's a knock on the door and my body tenses. Gabe must feel it.

"It's okay, babe. It's probably just Mel or Jack." Gabe gets up and goes to answer the door.

I don't even have time to turn when I hear footsteps run towards me. Mel's on me in seconds. "Are you okay? What happened? I wanted to leave work as soon as I got your message, but there was no one to cover. Shit, Belle. Why now?" Mel takes a breath and slumps on the couch.

I grab Mel's hands in mine and take a deep slow breath. "I'm okay, Mel. I think Mike's been playing Knicky Knicky on my door, and he called me."

I see Mel bite her lip, and I know she's freaked out. My strong friend is scared. She knows everything that happened to me, all the therapy I went through, and was strong through it all for me. But now, with eight years of freedom from that monster, I know she feels exactly like I do.

Scared to death.

I know there were charges on the other guys in the room for what they did to me as well, but they didn't stand trial for that, so I don't know the whole outcome to it. I just wanted it to all go away at the time. I assume since Mike went away that his friends did, too.

I'm in the middle of explaining to Mel about the phone call when another knock sounds on the door. My body tenses again. Fuck, will that ever stop? Mel and I both look to see who will walk through the door this time.

Gabe walks into the living room with a tall, lean man. He has shaggy brown hair and startling bright brown eyes. He wears a pair of dark wash jeans that hugged his body perfectly and a black t-shirt that shows off a set of tattoos on each of his arms. The man's definitely hot.

I'm not sure if I'm drooling, but my mouth's open. I hear a throat clear and I close my mouth, swallow deep and look to Mel who has an identical reaction to mine.

"Belle. Mel. This is Jack." I hear a chuckle come from both of the men.

I smile politely at Jack. "Hello, Jack. I've heard many things about you." I look at Gabe and smirk.

Gabe narrows his eyes at me and his lips are in a tight line—a look of warning about something...what I'm not sure, though.

I elbow Mel who seems to still be in a daze of some sort. "Hi," she squeaks out and blushes.

OMG. My friend blushed. She never does that. She must be really smitten by this man.

"Ladies," Jack speaks in a sexy, husky voice that I'm sure could melt any woman's panties.

The men walk towards the kitchen. Gabe speaks as he passes. "I'm going to give Jack the low down of the situation while you girls chat. We'll be back." Gabe smirks and then both men are gone.

When I look toward Mel, I see her still looking in the men's direction. I laugh. "Cat got your tongue, Mel?"

She immediately looks back at me with a huge grin. "He's fucking hot."

I laugh harder. That's my girl. Mel's back. "Yes, he sure is one fine specimen."

We can hear the men in the next room, but we can't make out words. Knowing that both the men are here to help out makes me feel even safer than I already did. I take a deep breath and relax.

"So anyways…" I continue to explain everything that has happened so far. Mel takes it all in. Beneath the fear she exhibits, the anger's there. I can see it. Mel doesn't like people hurting me and is always protecting me, too.

Mel leans in and pulls me in for a hug. I can hear her sniffle as she holds me, but I say nothing about it. I need to at least try to act strong, even though that's the last thing I actually am.

"Gabe will protect you." Mel mumbles through her tears. "And so will I! I'll do whatever it takes, Belle. You know I will." She pulls back, wipes her tears and looks at me. Such a brave woman she is.

I feel a little choked-up by her emotions and have to fight my own tears. "I know." I lick my lips and lean my head back on the back of the couch.

We sit in silence for a few moments, but they feel like hours. I'm not sure if I fall asleep or if I am just so deep in thought that I don't hear the men return to the room.

"You ladies want some takeout?" Jack's husky voice makes Mel open her eyes. She looks like she had fallen asleep.

I lift my head from the couch, turn my body and smile at Jack. I hear Mel mumble something as she stares at him openly. "That sounds great. I'm famished."

Mel clears her throat. "Yes, please," she manages to whisper.

My match-making thoughts begin to spin. I've never seen Mel react this way before with a man. I love it. I want to see her happy. All the men she has tried to be with have treated her like crap, and none of them were as hot as Jack.

Being the sweet, loving woman she is, I think Mel deserves to have a man treat her like a fucking princess. If I'm getting my fairy tale then Mel needs one, too.

I look back to Jack just as Gabe steps in front of me. He leans down and kisses my forehead. I blush, of course. I'm not used to all the public displays of affection, and with Jack being new to the fold, I can't help control my heated skin.

"Chinese or pizza, babe?" Gabe asks while he walks toward the kitchen. I, of course, tip my head to watch his behind as he walks. Damn. All the thoughts of match making sure put my mind in the gutter. I shake my head and smile to myself.

"Either one. I'm easy," I call out without even thinking about the words I am saying.

I hear both men chuckle. I scrunch my eyebrows and bite my lip in thought. It dawns on me. "Shit, Gabe. You know what I mean." I laugh and blush again. Then I tuck my head down to my chest and try to hide my embarrassment from Mel and Jack. Mel is used to my little quirky slips. I hear her laugh beside me.

"Yeah, Belle. I know, babe. Just not cheap, right?" Gabe laughs as he walks back into the room.

Ugh. Kill me now. He did *not* just use the rest of the phrase in front of his friend. Talk about total embarrassment. I pick up a pillow from the couch and cover my face with it. I can feel the couch cushions shake as Mel laughs. She has heard the expression on many occasions—it's an actual running joke between us at work when it comes to switching shifts. I just never expected Gabe to use it against me. I shouldn't have told him about it. What an evil, but loving, man.

CHAPTER 14

Belle

Gabe orders Chinese for dinner and tells us it'll be delivered in about half an hour. Gabe and Jack both get comfortable on the available chairs in the room and we wait.

Minutes pass and Jack stands. "I should get my bag from the truck. Best to start sooner than later," Jack says as he walks towards the foyer.

"Need a hand, man?" Gabe asks him while raising his eyebrows.

"Sure." Jack nods as he leaves the room.

Gabe gets up to follow him. "Be back up in a few minutes, ladies."

As soon as Gabe leaves the apartment I hear my cell ring. *I thought Gabe had my phone. Strange.* The sound comes from the kitchen. I set the pillow on the couch beside me and get up. I get into the kitchen and find my cell phone on the counter. It rings again. I look down at the display. It says 'unknown number' and that creepy chill races up my spine.

"Belle? Who is it?" Mel yells from the living room.

I slowly pick up the phone. I know I shouldn't, but I seem to be a glutton for punishment. I push all my fear aside and answer. "Hello?" I whisper loudly.

"Izzy's going to die." Next I hear a click and then nothing. He hung up. Tears well up in my eyes and my hands begin to shake. Hearing that old nickname has jolted fear right through me. I set the phone down on the counter and back up to the wall where I sink to the floor.

"Belle?" Mel yells again. I vaguely hear footsteps come into the room. "Belle?" Mel's voice muffles its way through the haze that's going on in my mind.

I stare straight ahead to the counter I just left my cell phone on. My hands still shake and goose bumps rise on my skin. My happy time from moments ago with Gabe, Mel and—I hope a new friend—Jack is gone. My past has come back to haunt me. The reality of the situation stares me in the face, and I don't think I can handle it. Everything crashes down so fast. Not once since I got that letter did I expect this kind of call, this kind of threat. I wish I could go back in time and never had met that bastard.

In the distance I hear Mel shouting out, "Gabe. Jack. Get your asses in here, now!" Then a herd of feet come running into the room. Voices call out to me, but I don't snap out of it. I'm in a fog, a deep daze of sorts. I am not sure I want to leave this space. It isn't real, is it?

I can feel my body as it lifts from the floor. I float, or at least it feels like it. By the smell of it, Gabe has me in his arms and carries me somewhere. Mumbles of voices continue. I hear snippets of the conversation, but not really. The fog is so thick that my gaze is blank. I don't know if I even blink.

I believe it's Mel's voice that speaks. "Phone ringing...floor-shaking..." Next thing I know, I'm set down, but not let go. Gabe still has ahold of me. Through the haze I can smell him. His smell is the only thing that attaches me to reality right now. Even though I don't want to be in the here and now, I won't let go. I won't give up. I haven't fought this long to be coward of sorts.

I feel the warmth of Gabe's body against mine and hear his heartbeat in his chest. I realize I'm curled into him. We must be on the couch because I can hear Mel and Jack as they talk with Gabe. The rumble of his voice soothes me to an extent. I know he's looking for answers and I just wish I was the one giving them. Soon I will be, but first I need to shake the fog that bogs me down.

"Has she ever reacted like this before?" Gabe's voice is muffled, but I can hear it clear enough as I sit dazed, listening.

CONTROLLING CIRCUMSTANCES

From a distance I can hear Mel. She's crying, but she answers. "This is how she was for days after the rape. All sense of reality was gone. It took a good week for her to shake it." Mel sniffles.

Gabe's grip on me gets tighter and then eases. I feel a warm touch to my head. He must've kissed me there.

It's hard to explain, the fog. It's not like the last time. I can sense and feel everything around me, but for some reason my body and mind don't allow me to respond. I suppose you can say it's shock, but not really. It's like I'm here and I *want* to answer Gabe when he speaks, but my mind just focuses on that phone call and the possible outcome. Maybe a wire is crossed or something.

Hands rub my back. It comforts and relaxes me. My body fights with my mind—fighting a battle to not give in, to not let Mike win. There's no way I will let that fucker win again. He took so much of me with him already. I can't let it happen again. I'm screaming inside, but no words come out. My lips are dry and unmoving. I stop listening to the conversation in the room. I can imagine they are looking for answers…answers only I can give.

I try to focus on the one sentence, the threat that caused this whole little meltdown. I force myself to concentrate. Gabe needs answers and I need to shake this and give him what he needs.

I feel tears begin to stream down my cheeks. Voices begin to become clearer. The words I wanted out finally slip through. "He's going to kill me." The words are shaky and my tone's low, but the words are out.

Suddenly, I shift in my seat to face Gabe. He stares at me intently. "What did you say?" he growls.

I blink a few times and wipe the tears from my face. Reality rushes back full force. I look at Gabe, lick my lips and swallow. "He said he was going to kill me."

Gabe pulls me into a tight hug and rests my head on his chest. "Like hell he will," Gabe grunts out. "Jack, get your computer running and let's get this shit started. No one, and I mean no one, is going to hurt my woman!" Gabe shifts on the couch. "You hear me, Belle? No one!"

Everything goes crazy at this point. Jack grabs his bags and pulls two laptops from them. He sets them on the table in the dinette space behind the couch. Mel gets up and rushes to the kitchen to grab my phone and hands it off to Jack. Gabe kisses my forehead and leaves me on the couch to watch the whirlwind occur before me. Cables are strung across the room from laptop to outlet. My cell phone gets plugged into an adaptor of some sort. I'm so not tech savvy, so I have no idea of what's going on. I just sit and watch. I wait and listen. Maybe they'll need me, maybe not.

Gabe brings me a glass of water and tucks a piece of loose hair behind my ear. He smiles a quick smile and crouches down in front of me. "Did he say anything else?" Gabe looks at me intently, expecting me to say more, but nothing else was said, so I just shake my head.

Gabe reaches out and gently takes my chin in his hand. He narrows his eyes. With tight, grim lips, he asks, "Are you sure? I need to know, Belle."

I blink away a lonely tear and shake my head again. "No. That was all."

Gabe straightens and walks back toward Jack who types away furiously on a laptop now. "Got anything, man?" he asks Jack with a low voice.

Jack looks up quickly with a grim expression on his face. "Nah, man. He's using a throwaway, so I can't get a return number." Jack looks back down to his computer. "I'm trying to ping the phone to see what towers he's hitting to see if he is in the area or not."

I watch Mel sit in a chair at the table with a mug in her hand. I'm not sure when she left the room to get a coffee, but I know with the look in her eyes that she means business. I can't wait to see the shit she'll put Jack through.

"So, Jack…" Mel makes the k louder than the rest of the name. Her eyebrows raise as she looks at him hunched over the computer, working away.

I snicker to myself. I knew it was coming. Mel's my best friend, but she can be a pain sometimes, especially when it comes to her friends. I pick up my water as I sit and watch it all play out.

Jack grunts, but never looks up. That man's going to push my girl and I'm going to get a kick out of it. It's nice to have something to distract me—at least for a moment or two.

Mel taps her nails on the table loudly and I smile to myself. "What's all this crap you have on the table here?" Mel asks as she takes a sip of her drink and sets it down. Then she leans forward. "I mean, what the hell will it do to help?"

Jack slowly looks up at her, a scowl on his face. "Crap? Are you serious right now?" He scoffs. "This crap," he chokes out his words, "is some of the most expensive, high-tech computer and software technology that the federal government uses to track down criminals." Jack sneers at Mel and looks down to his computer.

I can see the twinkle in Mel's eyes from where I sit. She's messing with him. Her shyness is gone and my brave friend is back and ready to play. I say bring it on, girlfriend.

The doorbell rings, which must be dinner, and Gabe heads down to get it. I'm not overly hungry now, but I know I can't become that sheltered woman I once was. I need to be strong. I head to the kitchen and hear someone follow. I look behind to see Gabe with a paper bag in his hand that smells absolutely divine. In the kitchen I begin to search cupboards for dinnerware to use when suddenly Gabe's hands wrap around my waist. I feel his hot breath on my neck. I close my eyes and take in his warmth. I love the feeling of Gabe against me. His breath on my neck teases me—I want his lips there. Anything to distract me from the situation I'm in, the reality of my hell that lies before me. I tip my head a bit and feel Gabe's warm, wet lips press lightly just below my ear. A soft moan escapes me. Gabe squeezes me tightly and whispers in my ear. "Are you alright, babe?"

"Hmm-mmm," I manage to get out.

Gabe's hand moves up my stomach, over my chest and to my neck. He turns my head perfectly so our lips can meet. Gabe's tongue slides across my bottom lip, and I moan again. This is the perfect distraction right now. My lips part for him and his tongue sinks in to meet mine. Our tongues and lips tease and tango for a few short moments before he pulls back, breathing heavily. I can feel his erection against my ass before he steps back.

"As much as I'd love to devour every part of your body right now, Belle, you need to eat and I need to help Jack," Gabe breathes out while he opens the bag of food on the counter.

How men can be so easily deterred, I don't know, but I'm feeling hot and heavy. I want to smack the man. I blow out a breath and glare at him. "Fine," I grunt.

Jean Kelso

After filling a plate with some chicken balls, rice and an egg roll, I head back out to the living room. Mel still stares intently at Jack as his fingers work furiously on the keyboard.

"Food's here, guys, if you want to eat," I tell them as I walk to the couch and sit down.

Both of them just nod in response. I smile at that.

I'm in mid-bite when Mel pipes up. "So are you in the FBI, Jack?" She pronounces the k loudly again. I almost choke on my food as I laugh.

"No!" Jack says firmly.

Mel starts to spin a piece of her hair around a finger, never dropping her gaze. "Are you secret service?"

I bite my lip to stop my laugh. Gabe walks towards me with a concerned look on his face. He holds a plate of food in front of him, but he doesn't comment.

Jack stops typing. He looks up at Mel tight lipped and stone faced. "No!" he says firmly, again.

I close my eyes and take a breath, my food all but forgotten. Shit's going to fly now. I know how my friend's mind works. I set my plate on the table and wait. Gabe sits beside me on the couch with his plate in his lap and starts to eat.

Mel shifts in her seat and leans right into Jack as close as she can. I see her bite her lip and her eyes sparkle with mischief. "Are you a terrorist?"

Jack slams his hand down on the table just as Gabe spits his food out of his mouth. I full out laugh because it's just hilarious how blunt Mel is being—no matter how stupid she is sounding.

"Jesus-fucking-Christ, woman!" Jack pushes his chair back and stands. His hands fly to his head and run through his hair. "Are you fucking kidding me right now?" He glares down at her.

Mel sits up straight in her chair with a huge grin on her face and the twinkle still in her eyes. She looks to me and winks. "Yep!" she says.

A growl sounds in the room. I look toward Jack, which is where the sound seems to be coming from. He has his eyes closed and shakes his head. "Fucking women!" He grunts and turns from the table. Jack stomps toward the kitchen, leaving Mel and the rest of us in the living room.

CONTROLLING CIRCUMSTANCES

Mel immediately stands, looks to Gabe and I, frowns and follows after Jack. I think she's going to do some groveling to make up to the man, especially if she wants in his pants.

CHAPTER 15

Belle

Everyone is done eating, the dishes are done and Mel and I are in the bedroom talking. The events of the day have taken a toll on me and I want to get washed and changed.

Gabe brought my bag into his room while I was doing the dishes and is now working on things with Jack, so it's girl time.

I step out of the bathroom after I wash my face and brush my teeth. Mel sits like a lump on the bed. "What's up, buttercup?" I move to sit beside her.

She looks up from her lap and gives me a small smile. "Just thinking of everything that could go wrong..." She scrunches her nose and pouts.

I sigh. I already feel slightly defeated due to exhaustion and then having heard the threat. "Look, I thought you were supposed to be the strong one, Mel." I give her a pep talk. "If it wasn't for you, I wouldn't have made it through shit the first time. I need you."

Mel blows out a breath. "I know. I'm trying, I really am, but when I saw you faze out like you did, everything came back, and I remembered how hard everything was back then." Mel shifts on the bed to turn her body towards me. "I don't want that bastard to get near you. If I could kill him and get away with it, I would. Christ, I wish he never got out of prison." Her shoulders slump with that final word.

Considering I'm the victim, I didn't expect to be the one consoling anyone. I reach out and pull Mel into a hug. I brush my hand over her head and whisper in her ear, "Me, too. Believe me, I feel the same way. Gabe says he won't let Mike hurt me, and I believe him. I need to trust that." Then my exhaustion takes over and the tears start again.

Mel and I both cry when the bedroom door slowly opens and Gabe peeks his head in. "Sorry to interrupt, ladies, but we may have got him."

This makes me sniffle back some tears and pull apart from Mel. We both straighten up and follow Gabe out of the room.

In the living room Jack still sits at the table. He smiles big and holds a beer. Once Jack notices me and my tear-blemished face, he turns to Mel and sees the same look on her face when his smile fades. "You ladies okay?" he asks.

I nod. "What did you find?" I ask as I sniffle back the remnants of tears and catch a whiff of the tasty dinner we had not long ago.

Jack set his beer on the table. "Well, I have good news and bad news. Good news is the ass-hat used his phone and I was able to track a signal when it pinged off of three surrounding towers."

"Okay…so what's the bad news?" I move to sit in a chair at the table beside him and try to look at the screen in front of him. None of it makes sense to me.

"Bad news is that the towers make up a triangle of a good hundred square miles, so he could be anywhere in that amount of space," Jack says.

I slump in the chair. That's definitely bad news. We know he's in the area, but we need to know where. Ugh, I just want to scream.

"But…" Jack perks up. "If Mike uses his phone for a longer period of time, I'll be able to actually trace his location. He wasn't on the phone long enough this last time, but at least we have an idea of where he is." Jack leans forward and takes hold of his beer. He takes a gulp. "Right?"

I look to Gabe and back to Jack. "So you're saying that we have to wait for him to call again and try to keep him on the phone?"

"Precisely," Jack answers.

I put my head down on the table and feel tears well up in my eyes. Why does all the shit happen to me? Why can't the bastard just leave me alone? I need air. I swallow the lump that forms in my throat as I sit up and look around. Gabe's not in the room. Jack types away on his computer. Mel sits on the couch and stares into space.

I stand up and mumble, "I need air." Then I wander to the foyer to slip on some shoes. Slowly, I make my way down the stairs and out the door.

The cool, fall evening breeze feels good on my hot tear-streaked face. I shut the door softly behind me and lean against the brick wall. I tip my head back and close my eyes. I rub the tears from my cheeks and wish things were better. I want my happy ever after, but at what cost? I slide my body down and sit on the cold pavement. The city's quiet considering the beautiful weather, but people still mill about the sidewalk. They pay no mind to little ol' me as I sit here. I tuck my legs up to my chest and wrap my arms around them. With my forehead down on my knees, I take slow, deep breaths to keep my anxiety at bay. The sounds of cars on the streets and feet walking by me compel me until I'm oblivious to my surroundings.

***

Gabe

I finish washing my hands and look into the mirror. Belle has dug herself so deep into my heart I don't think she'll ever be able to dig herself out. I see what this situation does to her and her friend and it makes me livid. I want to hurt someone or something. I'd prefer to hurt the bastard that she calls Mike, but I can't do that until we find him.

I take a deep breath and calm myself. I can't let the anger control me. Pleasure and pain go well together, but the pain I want to provide can't be combined with pleasure right now. I need to focus on Belle. I try to shake those thoughts as I dry my hands and leave the bathroom.

In the living room I see Mel on the couch. She looks like she's lost in her own little world.

Jack is in Ops mode. Jack's the man. If there's a friend in need—and Jack doesn't have a lot of 'friends'—he's there. Jack takes his work seriously and always makes sure there's a happy ending. I'm counting on him to get Belle and me through this. Actually, I'm counting on him to get me through this without me killing someone. Jack has seen my anger, and Lord knows how far I'll take it if this asshole hurts my woman.

I realize that Belle's not in the room. I don't hear any noises coming from the kitchen, and I know she isn't in the bedroom or I would've noticed her as I came out of the bathroom. "Where's Belle?" I ask Jack as I move toward the table.

Jack looks up with a puzzled look on his face. He looks around and shrugs. "I don't know, man. She was just here." He reaches for his drink and chugs back a sip.

I narrow my eyes at him. A deep, sinking feeling begins to rise in me. Where would she go? I look to Mel. "Mel. Mel! Where is she?" No response from her. The sinking feeling gets deeper. I slam my fist on the table to get her attention and yell, "Mel!"

Mel looks over at me. She shakes her head and blinks. "What?"

I blow out a breath. "Where's our girl?"

Mel looks around the room and frowns. "I don't know," she whispers.

I grip my hands in fists just as Belle's cell rings. All our eyes shift to it. It rings once. Then twice. The trace connects as I pick it up and answer. "Hello?"

"Izzy looks awfully lonely right now. She's just sitting out in the open, alone. It'd be so easy for me to just snatch her up," a guttural, snake-like voice says.

I grip the phone tightly. My anger rises, fast and dangerous. "Don't you touch her!" I grit out, but I'm not sure he hears it all since he hangs up. "Shit!"

Then the phone notifies me of a message. I look at the screen to see a series of photos. Belle sleeping on her couch. Belle and Mel leaving the hospital. Finally, a photo of Belle sitting outside my apartment. My whole body tenses. I toss the phone at Jack and run towards the door.

"I didn't get him, Gabe," Jack shouts to me as I move towards the door.

I quickly slip my shoes on and call over my shoulder to him. "He's fucking here watching her. He's been watching her for Lord knows how long. She's outside." I punch the wall in the foyer hard before I run down the steps to get my girl.

CHAPTER 16

Belle

Everything happens so fast. Gabe's door whips open and he comes running out. He looks around frantically. He startles me, and all I can do is watch him in dismay. Once he notices me sitting by the stairs, he reaches down and scoops me up. I wasn't expecting that. He catches me off-guard. I instantly wrap my arms around his neck and hold on.

"Fuck! Fuck! Fuck! Did he touch you? Fuck!" Gabe asks me.

I just smile at him in confusion.

Things continue to move fast. The scenery changes and then there's less noises. Up the stairs we go.

Gabe sets me on the couch and sternly orders me to, "Stay!"

I'm not going anywhere, but I need to know what the hell's going on. "What the hell, Gabe?"

Gabe walks back from the table with my phone in his hand. He sits beside me and pulls me into him. Then he blows out a long, deep breath. "You scared the shit out of me, Belle."

In complete confusion, I lean back and look at Gabe. Stress lines are noticeable on his face and his muscles are tense. I look around the room to Mel and Jack. They sit rather close and Mel seems upset.

"What's going on?" I ask everyone in the room. Gabe's upset, Mel's upset—geez—give me a clue, damn it.

Gabe asks me to look at him and he holds my face to keep my attention on him. His serious expression puts my nerves on alert, so I wait patiently.

"Mike's here, Belle," Gabe speaks intently.

CONTROLLING CIRCUMSTANCES

I try to pull back, but he won't let me. My now frightened mind can't think straight. "Where?" I ask.

Gabe leans forward and puts his forehead to mine. He breathes slowly and calmly as he speaks. "He's been watching you. He's been in your apartment and has been following you."

My body begins to shake. Shit. Mike has been this close, but for how long? He's been in my apartment and that means he was the one who opened the window. I swallow the hard lump in my throat before I grab onto Gabe and let my tears fall. "I don't want him to hurt anyone."

"Never!" Gabe growls. "He'll never hurt you or anyone else. I won't let him." Gabe kisses my forehead and pulls me into him, holding me close as my body shakes.

Finally, my body stops shaking. My nerves settle somewhat, and I look up at Gabe with a smile. "Thank you."

"Anything for you, babe," Gabe whispers as he runs his fingers through my hair—a gesture I love. It's such a relaxing thing to have done. Being cared for by Gabe like this and snuggling into his body heat, I let sleep take me…let it take my cares away.

CHAPTER 17

Belle

I wake to the sun shining brightly in the room. I vaguely remember sitting on the couch and being told that Mike has been watching and following me…being cared for by Gabe and then nothing. I fell asleep.

As I look around with my sleepy eyes, I see I'm in bed and only in a big tee shirt, which must be Gabe's. I pull the shirt closer and sniff. Mmm, it smells just like Gabe. I sigh and remember the situation I'm in. I toss the blankets aside and crawl out of the bed. I begin to move to the door. I hear voices coming from the living room—little snippets of male voices. I catch the odd word: trust, control. With those words I think I know what's being discussed—me.

I open the door and it squeaks just a little. I pad my way down the hallway. When I enter the living room everyone becomes quiet. Mel and Jack sit at the table drinking what I assume is coffee while Gabe heads in my direction.

"Belle, what are you doing up already?" He wears a frown on his face. Why is he upset? I have no idea.

"The room's bright. The sun woke me. What's the matter, Gabe?" I ask him and move closer.

Gabe takes me by the hand and tries to steer me back to the room, but I hold back. I stand firm and won't go anywhere. "Gabe."

"Belle." He stares at me with his eyes narrowed and his lips thin.

I raise my eyebrows and repeat myself. "Gabe."

He moves closer to me, eyes on me. "Belle…" I can see his eye twitch this time. Is he getting angry? Why?

CONTROLLING CIRCUMSTANCES

I return his stare, but don't speak. I won many staring contests at university, just ask Mel. She won lots of bets on them.

I'm not sure how long we stand there glaring, but Mel's giggle and Jack's husky voice break the showdown.

"For fuck sakes, Gabe. Don't be forcing her into shit. She doesn't want to lay down, don't make her. There's enough stress going around," Jack grits out.

With that I rip my hand from Gabe and look from Jack to Gabe. "Nobody is forcing shit. I do what I want." I stomp away from Gabe and head to the bathroom. I need a minute, and the last time I left the building shit hit the fan.

I slam the bathroom door behind me and move to the sink. Turning the water on cold, I lean forward to splash some water on my face. Gabe has been so good about not ordering me around, so why now? I may love him, but right now's not the time to push me. I'm not a fucking puppet.

I survived Mike once. I can do it again. I've managed to survive cancer so far, which was with the help of doctors and the support of my body. I can do this. I don't need Gabe if he's going to start bossing me around all the time. I take a deep breath and turn to the door. While I was fighting myself I must not have heard the door open.

Gabe leans in the doorway. He doesn't look happy, but he doesn't look angry, either. It doesn't matter to me at the moment. I'm pissed. My emotions are all over the place. "What?" I yell at him while I grab a towel to dry my face and toss it on the counter when I' done.

"Will you talk to me, please?" Gabe asks.

"I don't want to fucking talk to you right now," I yell again, letting my anger control the situation at hand.

Gabe doesn't move from the doorway. I want out of the bathroom, but I stand my ground. My heart begins to race with my anger. My breath grows heavy. I know if I don't calm down, my anger will turn to anxiety and then who knows what will happen?

"Belle, please calm down." Gabe softens his expression and stands straight in the door. I detect no more anger or frustration coming from him, but I don't know if I can trust that.

Gabe's right, though. I need to calm down. I close my eyes and try to take a breath.

Gabe catches me off-guard. Immediately and swiftly, he lifts me up and over his shoulder. I open my eyes to see his jean-clad ass. As much as his ass baits me, my anger isn't gone yet. Ugh. "What the fuck, Gabe?" I wiggle and begin to kick with my legs. A sudden smack to my ass that sits high in the air catches my attention. "Ahh! That hurt, fucker."

"You closed your eyes, babe. I took my chance. Now, we need to talk." Gabe smacks my ass again. "Now, shush, and no name calling." He turns us around in the bathroom, careful not to knock my body on the door frame, and walks us to the bedroom. I keep quiet as he demands.

Once in the room, Gabe kneels down and sets me on the bed. "Stay!" He leaves the room and returns moments later with two bottles of waters. Then Gabe shuts and locks the door before he comes toward me.

"Well, I'm here. Talk, Gabe." I huff. My anger subsides mostly. I feel defeat at best. I know Gabe has my best interest at heart, but damn it, he knows my past. I told him I wanted to try for him, but I won't tolerate being told what to do all the time. I cross my legs and my arms to wait.

Gabe hands me a bottle of water. Then he pulls the chair from the corner to sit in front of me. He looks at me, holding his bottle of water. A look of adoration and love glistens in his eyes, and a hint of hurt shows on his face. I sit there and take it all in. This gorgeous man sitting in front of me is mine. He swore to never hurt me, but with my past colliding with my present, my mind is a mess.

The silence. I can't stand it. Gabe just sits there and watches me. I look around the room, open my water and take a sip. "Well?" I ask sarcastically.

"Don't get lippy, Belle," Gabe says firmly.

"Well, you wanted to talk so talk," I tell him and slump my shoulders with a pout.

Gabe takes a breath, grabs my arms and pulls my hands into his. He holds them tightly. I try to pull them away.

"Let go, Gabe."

"No!"

"Yes!"

"Never," he growls.

96

I struggle, but he still doesn't let go. I have no idea why he won't, so I just give up with a huff.

"Look at me, Belle," Gabe demands.

I look up with a frown.

"How do you feel right now?" he asks.

He's seriously asking me that? "Frustrated," I tell him.

"Why?"

Is he being serious right now? "Because you won't let me go."

"I won't let go because I want you to know while I hold your hands, I have the control, and while I have the control, I need you to trust that I won't ever hurt you." Gabe stares at me intently.

This makes sense to me. He's trying to make a point. *Point taken.*

"Now, from a different point of view if not frustrated, how would you feel?" He gives my hands a squeeze.

I know I feel trapped, I think to myself. *When trapped and there's nowhere to go, one mostly feels helpless.* Like a light bulb switching on, I know this is what Gabe looks for. "Helpless," I whisper.

Gabe closes his eyes slowly and blows out a breath. "Yes. Helpless. That is how I feel."

I look to him, puzzled. Why does he feel helpless? "Why?" I ask him.

He finally let's go of my hands and sets them in my lap. Gabe sits back in his chair and speaks. "I feel helpless because I'm here with you, but I'm not really. I'm stuck standing on the outside looking in, watching you suffer from a past I can't imagine of what you endured." He runs his hands over his face and through his hair. After Gabe blows out a long breath, he continues. "I want to be the one to help, to help you escape that past and learn to trust the future that I hope we can have together."

My heart skips a beat. Things start to make a little sense. Just a little, though. Trust is a hard thing, and Gabe understands that. What I can't figure out is how his control issues will help. "I do trust you, but you can't control everything going on." I unfold my legs and set my feet on the floor. I lean forward as I look up at him and lick my dry lips. "I need to control my life. Having lost it once destroyed me. You need to understand that you can't have it all."

"I understand that. I really do. I don't want it all. I just want you. I can help you. You don't think I can see the anxiety, the panic that sits just under the surface? I can help with that. I want to help you with that. You just have to let me."

I love this man, I really do. I don't want to push him away. The help he offers is something I most likely need. I can't deny him. "Okay," I simply say.

"Thank, fuck!" Gabe growls. He lifts me off the bed and wraps my legs around his waist. I hold on tight, never wanting to let go. "We'll go slowly, but I know I can help you, Belle. Together we'll conquer this. I love you so much." He peppers my face with kisses as tears start to fall down my face, and I start to laugh.

"I love you, too." I give him a peck on the lips and hold him tight.

Gabe pulls back with a big smile on his face. His smile's worth seeing after seeing broody and bossy Gabe. I return the smile.

"Can I ask you something, Belle?" Gabe grins and raises one eyebrow in curiosity.

I nod.

"Has anyone else ever called you Izzy?" he asks. His expression becomes guarded. He probably expects the worst from me, but I only feel a quick thump of anxiety in my chest. I'm okay. Hearing that name is getting easier. In therapy years ago, my therapist called me that name to help me overcome the fear I attached to it. Believe it or not, it actually helped some.

I bite my lip and swallow the lump in my throat as I nod. "That was his name for me—only him. To everyone else I've always been Belle. I've never been a fan of it." I'm completely honest with Gabe. With trust comes honesty, right? "It used to be a trigger for me, but with therapy, things got better."

Gabe moves around the bed and lays me down. I release myself from him and relax into the bed. He lays next to me on his side. His arm wraps around my waist with his head being held up by his other arm. I turn my body slightly to face him.

"Speaking of triggers, my holding you down and restraining you I guess...when I kiss you, is that another trigger?" Gabe's eyes narrow. They hold many questions and possibly all the answers, too.

"It is, but as you say with your control and with me trusting you, it'll get easier. I'll overcome that, as well." I reach down and clasp my hand with his that lies on my waist. Hopefully, this talk with Gabe—touching him, reassuring him—will make it so he knows that I want him here, that I want his help and I just want him.

With my free hand I reach over to Gabe and run my fingers through his hair. I smile at him and lick my lips. I feel like I need to show him that I need him, want him and love him. I move my hand to the back of his head and pull him down to me. I press my now wet lips to his. My tongue licks his bottom lip and encourages him to open for me. Gabe does, and I slip my tongue in as I search for his. Once our tongues touch, sparks begin to fly. My need for him intensifies, and I don't think I can get enough.

I can feel the heat rise in me as Gabe shifts. His body slowly covers mine. Gabe's hands touch my body in just the right places. I begin to ache. I need him so badly. I reach my arms around his neck and pull him closer to push the kiss deeper. I want Gabe to know what I feel. I hope he feels it, too.

Gabe's kiss moves down to my chin and my neck to my collar bone. Little nibbles and sucks cause goose bumps to rise to the surface. Gabe's hand slips under my shirt and I feel him pull the cups of my bra down. Breast by breast, Gabe plays with my nipples. It causes me to moan under him.

He pulls back instantly and kneels while breathing heavily. "Shirt. Off. Now," Gabe growls.

My hormones rage, and there's no way I'll deny him or myself this. I reach for the hem of my shirt and begin to pull. I squirm and wiggle until I get the shirt up and over my head. I toss it aside and look to Gabe. His eyes are so dark, so intense looking. He looks like he's ready to devour me whole. Heck, I'm going to let him.

"Bra," Gabe growls while raising his eyebrows.

Talk about impatient. What am I talking about? If I could just snap my fingers and have us both naked, I would. God, I so would. These demands I can handle and meet. I lean up just enough to reach around and unclasp my bra and remove it.

Gabe is on me before the bra even hits the ground. His warm, wet lips wrap around my nipple. Gabe sucks while his hand caresses and tweaks the other breast. The sensations that roll through me are unbelievable. Feelings I want to feel over and over again with this man. I reach down and grab onto Gabe's shirt. I try to pull it up and off of him while he's occupied with little success.

Gabe grunts momentarily, leans back, pulls his shirt off and throws it off the side of the bed.

I lick my lips at him and reach for his pants.

Gabe smirks a sexy smile at me. He gets up from the bed. He's quick to remove his pants and mine. I giggle, but not for long. Soon my giggles are moans of lust and want.

"Stop teasing me, Gabe," I groan.

Gabe kisses my navel and moves downwards. It sends tingles of pleasure throughout me. Gabe's hot breath on my naked pussy makes me want to come already. I'm so worked up and I need him to stop teasing me.

Gabe's tongue swipes my clit and sends a jolt of extreme pleasure to my core. I try to lift my pelvis up, to grind my pussy to his face, but Gabe stops me. He holds me by my hips while he devours me and takes his fill.

I drive my hands into Gabe's hair because I need to grab onto something. The pleasure is unimaginable. Gabe sure knows what he's doing. He undoes me and puts me back together at the same time. A love I've never experienced and I don't ever want to lose.

"Ah, Gabe. Yes." I moan through every lick and touch he gives me.

My breath catches as Gabe pushes his finger deep inside me. I feel it curl just a little and can feel him hit my sweet spot. Gabe pulls his finger out and two go back in. I'm so ready to explode. Again, his fingers hit the spot. I can feel the tension build all the way from my toes up. "Gabe, I'm... ahh..." In and out a few more times with his fingers and deep suck on my clit. I'm a goner. I burst. The mind-numbing orgasm makes me scream Gabe's name and pull on his hair.

The bed dips and Gabe moves up and over me. I can feel his dripping erection at my opening. I'm beyond ready for him. He crushes his lips down on mine that drip with my orgasm, but I don't mind. I take Gabe's mouth and allow him to take control. In one quick thrust, he's in me and groans loudly.

"Fuck, Belle. I love you so much." Gabe pulls back slowly only to thrust forward faster and deeper. His hands roam up my ribcage, over my breast then to my hands. Gabe moves my hands to above my head and holds them there.

Even though I'm in a lustful daze, feeling the anxiety of being restrained can't be hidden. My body tenses slightly and I know Gabe notices.

"Trust me. I got you," Gabe whispers as he continues to hold my hands, removing one of his hands to leave both of mine in his one. He uses his free hand to caress my arm and then my breasts. Not once does he stop thrusting. Gabe brings me to another peak of orgasm. He kisses my lips and nibbles my ear and neck. He whispers continuously to me to reassure me. "I won't hurt you. Relax." *Thrust. Groan. Grind. Moan. Kiss. Thrust.*

I feel my body begin to tense again and wrap my legs around Gabe's waist to edge him on. So far, I'm doing okay being held by him. With Gabe reassuring me, it helps. My body relaxes and resumes accepting the pleasure it seeks. Score one for Gabe. Trigger, zero.

I can feel Gabe's body begin to shake and tense. He must be close. His breathing is heavy and he's getting really sweaty. I clench my walls around his cock to let him know that I'm more than ready.

"Gabe…oh—oh… I need to…" I pant.

Gabe thrusts deep and hard once, then twice. "Fucking come for me, Belle," Gabe growls and then he groans out his release as I scream out mine. Gabe bows his head into the nook of my shoulder and neck.

Gabe breathes heavily as he slowly pulls out and rolls to the side, releasing my hands. I move my hands down and lay them on my sweat-soaked belly.

I sigh contently. "That was amazing," I mumble while still coming down from my orgasmic bliss.

Gabe chuckles lightly. "Yes, it fucking was." He faces me and traces little circles on my arm. "So, are you okay? I mean, with how I held you?" he asks softly.

I close my eyes for a moment and gather my thoughts. This man just gave me two—count' em—two amazing orgasms, and he cares about me. Boy, do I love this man. "Hearing your voice helped a lot. Feeling you, knowing it was you, helped even more." I look into Gabe's eyes, which glistened with love that I return wholeheartedly, and smile.

CHAPTER 18

Belle

A knock on the bedroom door breaks our moment. Gabe reaches over and pulls a blanket over us. "Yeah?" he yells.

The door opens and Jack walks in a few steps. "Sorry to interrupt the love fest, but I think you need to come watch the news." The grim expression Jack wears means that it isn't good.

"Alright, give us a few minutes," Gabe tells him. Jack walks back out and shuts the door behind him.

Gabe tosses the blanket aside. Then he leans over and gives me a peck on the lips. Okay, time to get up. I roll to the side and am about to sit up when Gabe smacks my ass. "Hey." I wince just a little and then laugh.

"Opportunity knocked, babe." Gabe chuckles as he gets up from the bed and begins to pick up his clothes from the floor.

With both of us dressed and looking half-decent, I follow Gabe out to the living room. Mel sits on the big chair and cries while Jack stands behind the couch. He leans down and grips the back of the couch. What the hell is going on?

"Jack?" Gabe asks.

I go and sit on the couch. I look to Mel who in turn looks at me with red eyes and trembling lips. She nods her head towards the television. I turn to look. There on Gabe's TV a live news feed is on. They talk about a fire engulfing an entire building—something about arson. The volume is on low so I don't quite catch everything. I look to Mel and back to the screen. I don't understand. That is until a picture, a live feed of the fire, comes onto the screen.

I jump up from the couch. "Cock sucking, mother-fucker!"

Gabe watches me as I begin to pace the floor in the living room. Gabe looks a little confused about the situation, and since Jack doesn't enlighten him, I just blurt it out. "That rotten son of a bitch burned my place down."

Gabe turns to the television and growls. "Jack. We need to finish this." Gabe comes to me and takes hold of my shoulders. I look up at him and see the anger that seeps from him. If looks could kill, Mike's a dead man—but not before I get to him.

"I can't believe he did this," I cry out. I try my best to keep my anger at bay, but it's so hard. My heart begins to pound, and I fight to keep the tears back. "I hate him so much. He just keeps taking and taking. When will it end?" I grit out and look up to the ceiling. I can feel my body start to shake from the anger, the anxiety that wants to take over. How both of the emotions come together for me, I have no idea, but they do.

Gabe touches my cheek and brings me back to him. "Belle? You need to calm down. Take a deep breath. In through your nose and out through your mouth. You need to take control. Stay with me, babe. You got this. Focus." Gabe looks into my eyes and makes me focus only on him. He takes control of the situation at hand and helps to calm the anxiety that breaks at the seams to get out.

I do as Gabe tells me. I breathe in, and then out. I focus only on him. His simple touch keeps me in the here and now. "He isn't going to win, Belle. You have me. You always will."

I listen to Gabe's words and focus on my breathing. My muscles relax and my anger gives way. *Well, fuck. Gabe's good at this control stuff.*

I slump into Gabe's body and wrap my arms around him. I'm so thankful to have him by my side. I can still hear Mel crying over on the chair, so I release myself from Gabe and go over to her. I stand behind the chair and lean down to wrap my arms around her shaking form. "It's okay, Mel. I'm okay," I tell her.

Mel sniffs and reaches up. She takes my hands in hers. "I know, but what if you were in there?" She sniffles. "You weren't in the room. I was half asleep when the text came through and Jack turned the TV on. Seeing your home like that…" Mel blows out a shaky breath and continues. "I forgot you weren't there and just about freaked. If it wasn't for Jack reminding me you were here, I don't know what I would've done."

I give Mel a squeeze to let her know I'm here and not going anywhere. "I guess men are good for something, right?" I smile into Mel's hair. I know this will catch her off-guard.

Mel giggles and sniffs. "You jerk," she says. "Men are good for many things, and you know it."

This time I have to laugh. I kiss the top of her head and stand up. I look between the men and ask. "So what now?" I don't know if a plan of any kind will work or help to say the least, but I need to keep my mind occupied right now. I just lost my home—everything actually—and that stings like hell.

Jack finally sits down on the couch and Gabe leads me over there, too. He sits first and pulls me onto his lap. "Well, first we call the police about the fire. When we talk to them about that, we'll tell them our suspicions about Mike and everything else that has been going on." Gabe looks to Jack and Jack nods.

"Agreed. He's taking this to a whole new level and as much as we say we can protect you…I hate to say it, but I don't know if we can protect us all," Jack says to me before he glances at Mel, who's now curled-up into a ball on the chair, listening. "But first, I think everyone needs a good night's rest. I don't think I'll leave and go to the hotel tonight. If you don't mind, I'll crash here." Apparently, Jack had been staying in a hotel not far in another part of the city when Gabe called, so we had lucked out on him being so close by.

"Yeah, no problem," Gabe responds.

"Okay, good. Gabe if you want to make the call then take your woman to bed. I'll make sure everything is locked up tight here and set up some cameras for surveillance. Mel you can take the spare room, and I'll sleep on the couch out here." Jack takes charge of the situation—*and here I thought Gabe was the control freak.*

Jack hands Gabe his cell and Gabe makes the call. I tune out the conversation and think about everything that has happened so far. I pray that nothing else bad happens. When I tune back in, Gabe hands the phone back to Jack. Gabe begins to stand while he holds me in his arms. "A detective will be by in the morning to talk to us. For now, everyone get some shuteye." Gabe nods to Mel and Jack before he carries me to the bedroom.

Gabe sets me on the bed and goes to the window. He locks it and closes the curtain—not that it'll make a difference being a sheer fabric. Then Gabe goes to his dresser, grabs a pair of pajama pants and proceeds to strip out of his clothes. I can't help but stare. He's such a beautiful man, and I'll never get enough of him. As for now? Yes, I've had enough. The events of the day are finally catching up with me. The amazing sex, the fire, my anxiety—I'm exhausted and didn't even realize it.

I stand from the bed and go to my bag. I pull out a pair of pajamas and shyly begin to strip out of my clothes. I can feel Gabe's eyes on me and I blush.

"You best be hurrying with putting those pajamas on, Belle. I don't know how strong I am," Gabe growls.

Well, does that make a person feel wanted or what? I hurry to put my clothes on and turn to move toward the bed. Gabe is already in the bed. He holds the blanket back for me to crawl in. Well, isn't that sweet.

I do as invited and lay my head on his welcoming chest. Gabe wraps his arm around me and pulls me close. He kisses the top of my head as I snuggle close getting comfortable. "Good night, Belle. Sleep well," I hear Gabe whisper.

"Night, Gabe. Love you." I kiss his chest and close my eyes.

CHAPTER 19

Gabe

I wake long before Belle. Being restless through the night didn't help with sleep much. It was seeing those photos of my woman coming from that wretched man—if you can call him a man—and then hearing about him burning down her home. My thoughts ran wild all through the night. My need to kill the man is strong, but my love for Belle is stronger, deeper. If all I can do is try to keep her safe, then that's what I'll do...even if it takes my life to do it. The poor girl has been put through the ringer by this asshole, and I won't let him hurt her anymore.

I shake myself from the thoughts as I go to the kitchen to make some coffee. Today will be a long day, I know it. Jack is still asleep on the couch and the apartment's dark. I don't bother to turn on lights along the way. In the kitchen I turn the light above the stove on and begin to make a pot of coffee. I lean against the counter and think to myself of the things I plan to say to the detective when he gets here later this morning. I thought Jack and I could handle the situation, but I was wrong. Getting the police involved is the only option we have. I only hope that with their help that we can get the son of a bitch.

I want Belle to feel safe again. I want her to be able to live without fear. While Mike's still in her world she'll never feel that way. I'm only a man. I can only do so much, but I'll do everything in my power to help her.

I think about when I showed Belle the handcuffs and sex toys. I remember the glint and slight interest that she showed. After getting

106

to know her—seeing and experiencing what she's going through—she's more important than that stuff. Maybe later down the road when Belle feels safe and things are good we may play, but not now. We have our whole lives ahead of us, right?

"Is that coffee I smell?" a very tired-sounding Mel asks and startles me out of my thoughts.

I nod and smile at her. "It sure is. Should be ready shortly."

I open a cupboard, pull out a couple of mugs and set them on the counter. "Cream?" I ask.

"Please." Mel yawns as she stands in the doorway.

I gather the cream and sugar and set them by the mugs. "Help yourself," I tell her, then proceed to open a loaf of bread and pop down two slices in the toaster.

I watch Mel fix her caffeine fix and get at least her first sip in. "Are you doing okay?" I ask.

"Hmm, yes." She sets her mug down on the counter. "I'm a bit rattled, but I'm more worried about Belle. I was by her side when she went through the aftermath of the rape and trial, so I know the hell she went through. It was tough and she didn't handle it well." Mel looks down and fiddles with the hem of her shirt.

My toast pops, but I ignore it. "How do you mean?" I ask. This information intrigues me.

Mel reaches over to her coffee and takes a sip. And then another. "Well, she was afraid to go anywhere for the first little while. Every noise she heard, she thought someone was trying to get in the house to get her. When I did get her out of the house, if any man looked at her, she thought they were going to hurt her. And after the trial…" Mel pauses.

I move closer to her. I don't know if it's some secret she's about to share or what. I need to know. "After the trial what?" I urge her.

"After the trial, as Mike was being removed from the courtroom, he yelled to her that he was going to kill her." Mel grimaces. "I had to bring Belle to therapy every day. Everywhere she looked she thought she saw him. He was like the ghost of Christmas past, present and future. There was no escape for her and thought she was going to die."

"Well, shit. No wonder she's so hard on herself. The anxiety makes complete sense now." I shake my head in disbelief. I can't imagine what life was like for her then. That bastard needs to pay.

"The therapist put her on some medications and Belle had all kinds of counselling sessions. It was so hard to break her out of her shell, to prove to her that Mike was behind bars and that no one was out to hurt her. It took years, actually. When you started asking about her I was scared at first, but then I thought why the hell not? You know what I mean?" Mel grins at me.

"Thanks for the vote of confidence." I smirk and grab the now cold toast to toss it in the garbage. I make a cup of coffee and head into the living room. Time to wake up the house.

***

Belle

I wake to quiet chatter in the living room and toss the blankets off of me. I roll out of the bed and search through my bag until I find a pair of blue jeans and black tank top to put on. I'm not quite awake yet, so I'll give up my shower for coffee. I want to be able to think clearly about last night's events and discuss our next actions with Gabe and Jack. I know Mel will want to be in on the plan, but I don't want her to get hurt. Hell, I don't want anyone to get hurt. I just want to go back to sleep and forget any of this is even happening, but I can't because it *is* happening. This is what my life has become. Maybe my parents were right and it wasn't just the alcohol talking. Who knows? Maybe I *am* trash and not worth saving. Hell, what if Gabe can't save me regardless of all his heroic efforts?

I swipe the lonely tear that starts to run down my cheek and dress. These thoughts of worthlessness need to go. I try to keep in mind that Gabe and Mel both love me. They remind me all the time that I'm worth it. I head out to the living room. The men sit at the table, and Mel curls up on the couch and sips what I hope is a nice hot cup of caffeine.

I'm barefoot so no one hears me pad my way into the room. "I hope that's coffee you are drinking, and I hope to high hell that there is more where it came from." I lick my lips as I move farther into the

108

room. Everyone looks up at me, and Mel snickers as she nods her head.

Gabe raises his eyebrows at me. "High hell?"

"Uh, yeah?" I shrug as I move toward the kitchen.

Once in the kitchen I assume the empty mug by the coffee machine is for me, so I begin to prepare a steamy cup of caffeine for myself. Mid-pour I feel warm hands touch my shoulders and rub down my arms. Gabe's cologne or aftershave smells wonderful.

I set the coffee pot down and face him. "Morning, babe."

Gabe wraps his arms around my waist and leans us against the counter. "How are you this morning, Belle?" he asks with a hint of concern in his voice. Gabe's eyes full of pain. I know the situation is taking a toll on him. This is the last thing I want for him to deal with.

"I've been better." I'm not going to lie to him, but do I trust him enough to tell him how I really feel? I lean my head down to Gabe's chest and rest it there. I absorb his strength and debate on what I should do.

Gabe tips my head back up to look at him. "Belle, talk to me. I'm here for you, always. Let me in, let me help." He presses his forehead to mine and peers into my eyes. The truth shines brightly in his dark eyes.

I stare back and fight my internal battle. I know I can trust Gabe. Why am I finding it so hard to actually do it? He's been here for me through so much, has kept every promise to date and has held my hand through the toughest times. He hasn't run yet, so if he's willing to handle all that crap, then I suppose he isn't going anywhere.

Bound with determination about myself and with my mind made up, I let the words flow. "What if you can't help me? What if you can't stop Mike from hurting me, from getting to me?"

Gabe immediately steps back and grasps my upper arms. "Belle, I'll do everything in my power to protect you. You are…" Different emotions of pain and hurt flash across Gabe's face while Gabe's muscles tense. Suddenly, Gabe drops to his knee in front of me and wraps his arms around my legs. When Gabe looks up at me his eyes glisten. "You mean the world to me. If I can't do this myself, I'll get help. I know my limits."

Did I just break my strong, controlling man? He wanted me to let him in, and I did. This is what I get in return. I made him feel weak? Fuck. I look up to the ceiling and try to control my own emotions. I feel Gabe squeeze my legs to get my attention.

"Belle, I can do this," Gabe mutters.

I swallow back my sob and look down to him. "I didn't mean to make you think you weren't good enough, Gabe. I just meant that maybe you'll need more help than Jack. The two of you aren't going to be enough to take the psycho down." I bite my now trembling lip. "Look what he's done already. My home's gone. Mike was able to get that close and made me more vulnerable. Just imagine what else he could do. I don't want to lose you in process." Tears start to run down my cheeks now.

Gabe pulls me down to the floor with him. He sits up and pulls me into his lap. I sit so I face him and he wraps his arms around me. "Belle, you'll never lose me. You're worth everything to me. I'll do what it takes to stay here by your side through everything. You're one of the strongest women I've ever met. I'm honored to have met you and to have the chance to love you." Gabe sweeps his finger through my messy reddish hair then wipes away the tears from my face. "The strength you have has conquered more things than anyone person should have to in one lifetime. You're so brave and beautiful. You're worth *more* than everything in this world to me. Don't you ever forget it." He leans down to me and kisses my forehead. "I'm not going anywhere."

The wall I had built up for so many years completely crumbles. After all this time of being held behind that wall because of fear and shame, I now begin to feel whole. In the arms of this man, I feel like a real woman. I feel like I can be myself and that I'm loved. I'm not sure how to respond to Gabe after such a wonderful speech. My hearts beats fast and loud. I reach my hand up and caress his cheek. I lick my lips to moisten them from being dry, lean in and give Gabe a peck on the lips. Then I lean back and smile at him. "I love you so much, Gabe."

CHAPTER 20

Belle

Detective Douglas shows up at nine a.m. He looks freshly washed, but tired all the same in his pair of black slacks and a gray button-down shirt. Gabe offers him cup of coffee and we all sit at the dining room table.

Gabe wants to take charge of the situation, and since I have no clue on how to deal with everything, I have no problem with that.

Before Gabe has a chance to speak the detective jumps right in. "Ms. Jones." The detective sets his mug down on the table and looks directly at me across the table. "I reviewed your file last night and, first, I would like to apologize for what you had to endure in your past."

Feelings of shock come upon me. *An apology from a man who has nothing to do with the situation. How kind his soul must be.* "Thank you, Detective Douglas," I whisper.

"Gordon, please. I may be old enough to be your father, but I'm here to help." He smiles and takes a sip of his coffee.

I notice Gabe shuffles in his seat. I know he's ready to get this show on the road. I look towards him and raise my eyebrows while I smirk knowingly at him.

Gabe narrows his eyes at me and turns to look at Gordon. "So, Gordon. Do you have anything from last night that will lead us to anyone particular? Say a man named Mike?"

I sit back in my chair and watch the scenario play out. Man vs man. Gordon sets his mug aside. He reaches into the pocket of his shirt and pulls out a little notepad. Gordon flips it open and turns through the pages until he finds the one he wants. Gordon grimaces as he glances at Gabe.

Gabe leans forward in his chair and folds his hands on the table. He appears anxious. I'm not sure if Gabe wants to strangle the detective for answers or do something completely different. Reading male emotions isn't easy.

Dealing with my own emotions isn't easy.

"The fire chief and the inspector spent hours in the mess after the fire was put out." Gordon looks to me then back to Gabe. "They have deemed the fire arson, but so far there are no real leads as to who set the fire. I'm sorry."

I puff out a breath at the same time Gabe yells. "Fuck!"

"Keep cool, man," Jack pipes up.

I look to the other end of the table in surprise. I forgot that Jack and Mel were even in the room. They've been so quiet so far and that's just not normal for Mel.

"I'm cool," Gabe grumbles. "I'm fucking cool." I can tell Gabe's barely holding on. He wants answers and that isn't the one he wants. I reach over to him with my hand in hopes that he'll take a hold of it. I want to reassure him that I'm here, to reassure him that I'm safe. At least I am right now.

Gabe takes my hand and gives it a slight squeeze. "Gordon, I'm going to level with you." Gabe nods his head toward the little notepad that Gordon holds in his hand and takes a breath. "I have no idea what you have in that little notebook, but what I know, I don't like. Belle has suffered enough in this lifetime all because of this rotten bastard, and I want him out of our lives. I wanted him out of it yesterday!"

Gordon closes his notepad and shoves it back in his pocket. He leans back in his chair and crosses his legs. "From what I've read, I agree, but we have no proof he set this fire."

Gabe lets go of my hand and begins to stand. I hear a low growl start deep in his chest. Before I can speak up, Jack stands defensively as if to engage Gabe if necessary.

Gabe looks to Jack. "Sit down. I'm alright." Gabe begins to pace the room. He rolls his shoulders and flexes his fists. Suddenly, Gabe leaves the room, only to return moments later. His appearance has no change. The anger's still there, but there seems to be a subtle calm set upon his features.

Gabe sits back in his chair and leans forward with his hands clasped together in his lap. "Look, Gordon. I don't mean to be a prick, but I know this asshole set the fire. He's been harassing and threatening Belle for a while now. I won't let him hurt her anymore." Gabe narrows his eyes in the detective's direction. "You got me?"

I drop my head to the table with a bang. The way Gabe speaks to this man isn't the way you should be talking to a gentleman of the law. I clench my eyes shut and bang my head on the table once more. Things couldn't get more complicated.

"Belle, stop that," I hear Mel whisper.

I feel someone touch my shoulder. It's a touch of unfamiliarity, so I stop what I'm doing and sit up. It's Gordon. He removes his hand from my shoulder and looks me in the eye.

"Look, Belle, I understand where Gabe's coming from. If you were my daughter or wife, I'd be hell bent ongoing after the man responsible for the horrible things he did to you and apparently is still doing to you." Gordon glances towards Gabe and nods. "I'll help you in any way I can. Tell me what all has happened since this Mike guy was released from prison."

Gordon seems genuine enough—fatherly and honest. He sits in the dining room with the four of us as Gabe, Jack, Mel and I explain all the things that have happened in the past month or so. Gordon takes detailed notes and gives us safe ideas on how to go about handling the whole situation legally.

When Gordon mentions the word legal, I notice a glint in Gabe's eye. As if I didn't know already, anything legal about this situation has already gone out the window and Gabe's beyond game about it. Maybe now that Gordon the fatherly detective is willing to help, Gabe can contain himself and keep himself safe in the process, too.

By two in the afternoon the group of us are starving. Gordon needs to head out because he has another case that he has to look into. He bids us farewell and promises to call if he finds any leads.

Jack leaves to go to his hotel. He plans to get his stuff and check out. Jack will stay here at Gabe's until this is over. Mel decides to go with him and says they'll pick up some pizza on the way back.

I need a bit of stress relief, so I lock the door and lead Gabe towards the bathroom. A shower is always stress reliever, and Gabe in the shower with me will be an even bigger stress reliever.

As I gently—but persistently—push Gabe into the bathroom, I caress my hands up under his shirt. They roam along his hard abs, up his chest and back down. Gabe stops and turns in my arms with a mischievous look in his eyes. A sexy smile forms on his face, and I know that he knows where this is heading.

I go in with control. I want to offer some relief, but knowing how I feel for this man and knowing how he makes me feel, I let my control go. I love this man and I'll give him anything. I want to give him the world just like he says he wants to give it to me. I've always wanted to have control in my life since that day—always needed it--but with Gabe there's no need. He's my control. He's my power, my salvation to this life. He'll keep me afloat, alive. He'll keep me breathing when I don't want to be breathe anymore. I thought I had only one life to live, but I was wrong. I have two lives to live. One for me and one for Gabe. Together—two lives lived as one. He *is* my one. My whole.

I push Gabe's shirt up over his head and drop it to the bathroom floor. Looking deep into his eyes, I force him to see all of me. Then I drop my arms by my sides and stare. I wait. I wait for him to accept all of me. He doesn't disappoint me.

CHAPTER 21

Belle

We share no words verbally. Our eyes say it all—our hands, our lips, our tongues. Gabe swoops in and wraps his arms around me, pulling me closer as he crushes his plush lips against mine. I feel his tongue sweep along my lip and try to gain access. Who am I to deny? I open willingly and his tongue invades my mouth. I thrust my tongue against his and passion takes over. Heat begins to rise from the tips of my toes and into my chest. Our lips never lose their lock as I feel Gabe pull at my clothing and tug it off. My shirt rips—my poor little tank top. I won't miss it, so it is ok. Next, down go my little shorts. Goose bumps rise on my flesh. Gabe's hands are everywhere, or at least they feel like they are everywhere. I can feel everything. I'm beyond open to his touch—I *want* to feel everything. He pulls back and looks into my eyes. Lust dances in the depths of Gabe's gaze. He reaches for the waist of his jeans, unbuttons them and shoves them down. Once he kicks them aside, I pull his leg between mine and move my legs apart. Gabe moves closer to me so he stands between my legs. Then he lifts me onto the vanity and leans into me. Gabe begins to suckle on my ear and throat. He nips and licks his way down my neck and the sensations drive me wild. I tip my head back as I feel shivers of pleasure begin throughout my body. Gabe's hands begin to glide up my legs, from calf to thigh to hip. His touch is gentle and loving and I want more. I feel a hand move up my stomach and glide up to my breast as the other hand slowly caresses its way to my core. His strong, long fingers begin to rub up and down my wet crotch. I feel like I'm ready to come already. How? I don't know.

My breathing increases. My mouth begins to get dry. I lick my lips and look to the object of my desire. I reach my hands out and begin to rub my hands through his messy—but sexy—hair and pull him in for a kiss. I hear him groan.

"You're so ready for me," Gabe growls as he slips a finger into my dampness. I can't help but moan.

"Yes!"

"This is mine. I'll protect it and you with my life." Gabe thrusts a second finger in as he kisses from my lips to my ear and down my neck, heightening the pleasure I already feel.

"Yes!" I feel lost to him, to his touch, to the pleasure his lips and hands are giving freely to me. I want more. I won't ask, I won't beg. He knows I'll take what he'll give. My body responds with a shiver and my hips move into his thrusts on their own. My body knows what it wants and seems to have no shame in showing Gabe. Thrust after thrust. Moan after groan. I can't take it. I need more. "Please, Gabe." Here I said I wouldn't beg. I guess I was wrong.

"You ready for more, babe?" Gabe groans as he slips his fingers free from my wet folds and begins to stroke himself. My eyes are instantly drawn to his erection. He's so hard and large. We have had sex on several occasions, so I know how Gabe feels inside of me. I feel so aroused and I want him—now.

I reach down to Gabe's hand that is stroking his erection—a hint given to what I want. Gabe grabs my hand and places it on the vanity. "Keep it there!" he orders. He reaches up and grabs my other hand to repeat the action on the other side. Another shiver overcomes me. Gabe then takes ahold of both my hips and drives himself in. He thrusts balls deep inside of me and my head falls back and hits the mirror. I want to scream because it feels so good, but when I open my mouth only a deep, sated moan comes out. Gabe pulls my hips closer to his and grinds his pelvis against me. He pulls back slowly and says, "I love you Belle."

He thrusts hard again and again and again. Thrilling sensations swim through my body and my toes begin to curl. A tingling sensation begins in my stomach and my core begins to spasm around Gabe's cock. He hits every sensitive spot possible and I love it.

"Oh my fuck, Gabe." I grip the vanity and close my eyes tight. What I want to do is wrap my arms and legs around him, but he tells me no. I'll be a good girl, but only for him. It's all for him. I love him. "I'm...I'm...Fuck... ahhhhhh" And the biggest orgasm I've ever had blows through me.

Gabe thrusts once, twice, a third time and then directs me to wrap my legs around him. He swoops me up from the vanity which gives me no choice but to wrap my arms around his neck now. He turns immediately and slams me against the wall where he thrusts a few more times. "You will be mine until the end of time." Gabe grunts then stills as he moans out his release and holds me up against the wall.

He stands quietly, breathing heavy for a few minutes, just holding me while he is still inside of me. I can feel his and my own cum begin to ooze out around his slowly fading erection.

I rub his back and kiss the side of his head. "Shall we shower now?" I whisper to him with a big smile on my face. I still feel high, feel the rush of the orgasm flowing through me, but I know we don't have a lot of time before Mel and Jack get back with food.

"Yeah," Gabe mumbles. He steps back from the wall and pulls out from me. He slowly sets me on my feet. Gabe kisses my forehead before turning toward the shower and turning it on. Is our moment over?

Gabe turns and reaches his hand out to me. I accept. As I walk towards him I feel a heat surge through me at the thought of the unknown. The connection we share, the feelings we explore on a daily basis is a wonder to me. It's something I never expected to ever have.

This man is it for me. He is him. He's the one. Why I ever fought it, I'll never know. Now we just need to get through this mess I've managed to get us in and maybe I—or shall I say we—will get a fairy tale ending.

Gabe grasps ahold of my hand and pulls me into the shower under the hot water. He wraps his arms around my waist and pulls our bodies tight together. We let the water just run over us. I look up to him and smile. "I love you, Gabe."

Gabe reaches a hand up and pushes a strand of loose hair behind my ear. He returns my smile and licks his lips. "And I love you, my sweet girl." Gabe leans down and kisses my lips gently enough to feel the warmth of his touch.

Twenty minutes later—after Gabe generously washed me from head to toe and I courageously did the same for him— we dress and sit on the couch as we wait for Jack and Mel.

CHAPTER 22

Belle

Jack returns to the apartment carrying a large duffle bag on one shoulder and a large briefcase in his other hand.

Mel follows with two boxes of pizza and backpack that probably carried her basic essentials.

Bags are set by the couch and the pizza on the table.

Gabe heads in Jack's direction, and I head in the direction of food. Believe it or not, sex—and I mean good sex—brings on a good appetite.

I grab the pizza and bring it to the kitchen. I open the cupboards and take out some plates. I set them on the counter. As I reach for the paper towels I shout out, "How many slices do you want, guys?"

"We're coming, babe," Gabe calls back from the other room. I shrug to myself and plate two slices of pepperoni. Next I rip off a piece of paper towel and go back out to the living room.

"Get it while its hot, guys." I smile and curl up on the couch. Mel comes and sits beside me with her own plate of yummy deliciousness. The pizza smells so good. I can't help but dig right in.

As I take a bite, I hear my cell phone ding. I look around the room and spot it on the side table. I reach over and picked it just as Gabe shouts, "Don't touch it."

I was just a little too late. I answer accidently and get the shock of my life.

"You're going to die tonight!" the voice tells me.

I drop the phone. I drop my pizza. It feels like my heart stops right then. Gabe's by my side instantly.

"What is it?" Panic and worry are etched on his face and in his voice.

I feel the blood drain. The color of my face pales as I look at Gabe. "I... I..."

Gabe pulls me into a bear hug. "You're safe, Belle. He won't get to you. Jack and I have somewhat of a plan."

In my peripheral vision I can see Mel setting her plate on the table. Tears shimmer in her eyes. "This has to end now," Mel says. "This is killing her and it's hurting me as well. I can't stand seeing this all going on." Mel looks to me, Gabe and then to Jack. "What's the plan?" She sniffles.

"Let's all eat something first, then Jack and I will lay it all out," Gabe says before he lets me go to stand up. Gabe looks at me once more before he walks to the kitchen. Jack follows.

Mel blows out a breath, picks up her plate and begins to eat her pizza. I pick up my plate and pizza from the floor and set it on table. I'm in no mood to eat now. There's something about getting a death threat that deters your appetite.

Gabe and Jack return to the room with plates loaded full of pizza. They sit in the empty chairs, eat and make small conversation. Gabe doesn't seem too happy that I'm not eating, but tough shit for him. He's not the one under a death threat. But then again I'm not about to tell him that. I just smile politely at him and listen as they all talk.

When everyone finishes eating and the dishes are set aside, it's time for the big talk.

Jack brings around the briefcase and opens it up. He pulls out little bits of equipment that look like every day knick-knacks. I scrunch my eyebrows in confusion because I have no idea of what's going on. Are we going to sell shit? Is this the hair brain scheme?

Jack notices my confusion and decides to enlighten me. "These are cameras." He smirks. "We plan to set these up around the apartment to monitor every room from several angles." He looks from me to Mel.

Mel speaks up first. My girl seems to be done with the tears for the moment and ready to fight back. But she needs to know how. "Why do you need to monitor the rooms?" she asks.

Gabe leans forward in his chair and looks from me to Mel. He clears his throat, licks his lips and looks back to me. "As much as I really hate this plan, Belle, Jack and I feel this is the best idea. You and Mel will be bait."

I don't let Gabe finish his thought. He wants us to bait for that animal? How? Why? Is he trying to get us killed? He swore to me he was going to protect me and dangling me out there for the fucking wolf would guarantee my death. Ugh. "What?" I yell as I jump up from the couch. "You plan to dangle me like fresh meat for a wild animal? How dare you?" I'm outraged. I start to stomp out of the room when Gabe wraps his arm around my waist.

"Belle, wait. Please," Gabe pleads. "Please listen to the whole plan. Listen to what Jack and I have planned out."

I close my eyes and take a deep breath. I trust him, I do. I just don't know what all Mike's capable of. What if this so-called plan fails? What something happens me or to Mel? Will Gabe or Jack be able to live with themselves? I turn into Gabe's arms and look up to him. "Okay, tell me." I have to believe he'll keep me safe. I need to believe Jack will keep Mel safe. If he doesn't I'll rip Jack's nuts off and shove them down his throat. Ugh. I move to sit back on the couch. Gabe sits back in his chair.

Between Jack and Gabe the plan's explained. They hope to set Mike up with using us girls—well, mostly me—as bait. With the camera's they plan to survey the apartment, as well as watch and record everything that happens. We just pray that Mike isn't too many steps ahead of us. Hopefully, he's not smarter than what he used to be. The men plan to leave us girls alone in the apartment and watch us via video on a laptop. Now that we have Gordon on our side, it's a major bonus. As long as everything goes as planned, catching Mike in action and with our testimonies should put him back in jail. Hopefully, for a really long time.

"Now, we just need to pick when we plan to follow through with this," Gabe says. "We'll never know when Mike plans to strike next and—"

I interrupt Gabe by clearing my throat. "Uh, yeah we do."

Gabe turns to me with confusion clear on his face. "What do you mean, Belle?"

I cross and uncross my legs, then shift my body on the couch and blow out a breath. "The phone call from earlier…it was Mike."

Gabe moves in front of me and kneels down. "What did he say?" He takes hold of my fidgeting hands.

"He…uh…said I was going to die tonight," I whisper and look away from him.

Gabe reacts instantly. He lets go of my hands before he jumps up and yells. "Fuck!" He runs his hands down his face. As he begins to pace the room, he starts to grunt out orders to Jack. "Jack, we need to get the camera's set up, now!"

"On it!" Jack replies and gets up from his chair. He begins to strategically place the knick-knacks around the apartment.

CHAPTER 23

Belle

It's eight in the evening and the apartment has been wired to videotape from every possible angle. The men just left with hopes of being able to sneak in the back way to the bar and set up Wi-Fi to watch live feed of the video. Gabe told us to act as if nothing was going on, to act as if Mel and I are just having a girls' night in, so Mel is popping popcorn in the kitchen and I'm now trying to decide on what to watch.

"Want extra butter, chick?" Mel shouts from the kitchen.

"Is that even a question?" I laugh as I shout back. I scroll through the Pay-Per-View list and see that there are a few movies that sound pretty good. I don't know when Mike plans to show face—if he even plans to. I decide against having alcohol. My emotions are frazzled and I really could use a drink to help keep me calm, but alcohol could mess up my judgement, and I don't want to ruin anything that could possibly happen tonight.

Mel walks into the living room carrying a big bowl of delicious smelling popcorn with a smile on her face and comes to sit on the couch beside me. I know this situation doesn't bode well for her, but she puts up a good front just like I do.

"So what have you picked?" Mel tosses a few pieces of our snack in her mouth and looks to me.

I'm so thankful to have Mel by my side and to have her as a friend. I know she's doing this for me. Mel's putting herself in harm's way when she doesn't need to. I look to her and just stare for a

123

moment. My heart beats a little fast and my emotions swell as I look at my best friend. She's always here when I need her. How I lucked out with such a person in my life, I'll never know, but I'm thankful for sure. Tears begin to form in my eyes.

Mel's smile drops as I'm sure she notices my mood change. "Are you okay, Belle?" She sets the popcorn on the table and reaches for my hand. "Everything will work out you know. The guys will keep us safe."

I hold her hand in mine and wipe the tears that spill from my eyes. I need to get a grip, I know, but I need to tell her my feelings before anything happens. "I love you, Mel."

"Oh, sweetie. I love you, too." Mel squeezes my hand.

I smile as a few more tears leak and stream down my face. "You're the best friend any girl can have. You've been by my side through so much, and I just want you to know that it means the world to me to have you in my life." I lean forward and pull Mel into a hug. I squeeze her tight and can feel her body begin to tremble. Her emotions have probably let loose.

"I think I'm the lucky one," Mel mumbles against my neck.

I pull back to wipe my tears and so does Mel. We both smile and sit back on the couch. "So how about that movie?" I ask.

***

Gabe

After we leave the girls, Jack and I walk around for a bit. We stop in a coffee shop and grab a cup to go before we walk a bit more. I want to try to show that we are not going back to the apartment in case anyone's watching. I have a back entrance to the bar that I can get to from the street behind, so if we work it right we'll be able to sneak in without being noticed.

Once at the bar Jack gets down to it. He heads to my office and gets the laptop he knows I keep there for work and brings it back out. He sets it on the bar, opens it and turns it on. Then he pulls out an USB stick from his pocket. Soon the Wi-Fi is set up and we gain access to the live feed from upstairs.

CONTROLLING CIRCUMSTANCES

I lean against the bar top and watch as the screen brings up several feeds. Each room has at least two cameras, just at a different angle. Jack still taps at keys on the keyboard and as he does, I notice a red light in the corner of the screen come on. I'm so glad I closed the bar for the night. I don't think I could focus on the task at hand with a busy bar to run, too.

"What's that light?" I ask him.

"It means all feeds are recording," Jack answers.

I nod. "So anything that happens in the apartment will be seen and recorded?" I ask.

"That's the plan." Jack says as he taps the last key and looks to me.

I watch the monitor for a minute and nothing seems out of the ordinary. The girls are in the living room watching something on the television and it looks like they are snacking on something. Everything seems calm at the moment.

I pull my cell out of my pocket and call Gordon. He's in on the plan and so is his department. Gordon will meet us here at the bar. I wonder where he is.

A knock at the back door sounds just as I start to dial. I pause and go to the back to let Gordon in.

Gordon is dressed as if on the clock with badge and gun holstered at his waist. We head to the front of the bar. "Sorry I'm late," Gordon says. "I wanted to make sure my men were set in case things went down." He sits on a stool by Jack at the bar. "Anything yet?"

Jack looks up from the computer and nods to Gordon. "Hey. No, nothing yet."

I grab stool and pull it around the bar to sit down across from the other men. "So I guess we just sit and wait?" I ask them.

"We do," Jack answers. "Now, are you going to serve us beverages or what, man?" Jack looks to me with a smirk and nods toward the bottles of whiskey behind me.

"None for me," Gordon says. "On the job, remember? But I would take a soda or water."

I know Jack likes his whiskey neat, so I go about pouring him a glass. I grab a bottle of water for Gordon and one for myself. I want to stay clear-minded in case something does happen. Deep in my gut I know Mike will make his move tonight, and I want to be ready.

With drinks in hand we sit on our stools. We all watch the monitor and wait.

CHAPTER 24

Belle

I pick a comedy to watch with hopes to keep Mel and me both from thinking. I want us to relax and laugh a little. I think it's working, with Channing and all his sexy glory acting as an undercover cop pretending to be a college student, but when I began to hear footsteps in the ceiling, the hairs on my arms stand on end. My muscles all tense up and I look to Mel.

"Do you hear that?" I whisper. I see Mel is tense, too. Her whole body seems stiff and her eyes slowly wander around the room.

"Yes," she says back softly.

"Okay, we're supposed to remain calm, right? Fuck, how do we remain calm? Does Gabe have an attic?" Fear begins to creep in. All of my rational thoughts begin to slip.

"Shh…" Mel mumbles. "Relax or I will start to flip out."

I take a deep breath and try to gather myself. More footsteps sound and a shiver crawls up my spine. I curl my fingers in a fist and squeeze to try to contain the fear. "Okay. Sorry," I whisper again. I don't really know why we're whispering, but if it helps to keep both of us somewhat calm then I suppose whispering is what we'll do. I'm not sure if the cameras that are set have microphones or not, but I don't really care either. The police only need visual proof of an attack—at least that's what Gordon said to me.

I survived Mike once and I can survive him again, right? I also just beat cancer, so there's no way I'm going to let Mike beat me. I need to shake some of the fear off and pull my big girl panties up. Gabe isn't here right now. He can't protect me. I'm bait. Mel's bait. Shit, my mind is wandering. I shake my head to clear my thoughts and look to the television.

The footsteps stop and so do my thoughts. Mel grabs for my hand to get my attention I assume. "You want a drink, hun?" she asks.

I look to her and scrunch my nose up. Why would she be asking that? Someone is in the fucking ceiling. I'm going to die tonight and she wants to know if I want a drink? I stare at her. She stares back.

"Belle? Belle?" Mel shakes the hand of mine that she holds. "I'm thirsty and getting a drink, do you want one?" She glares at me as if I should know what she is talking about. I look to the kitchen and back to her. Is there part of the plan I missed? No, there isn't. I know there isn't. She seriously just wants a drink. Suddenly, it dawns on me. We are supposed to act normal, not do anything suspicious to cause Mike to change up his plans for the night. Boy, do I feel stupid.

"Yeah, sorry. I would love a glass of soda. Thanks," I tell her and smile.

Things have been quiet except for the movie for the past half hour. No more footsteps or any other noises have occurred. Maybe Mel and I are just losing our minds. I try to relax and pull the blanket from the back of the couch. It's the blanket I brought from my place to make me feel more at home here. I cover myself up with it and lean against the end of the couch. I try to pay closer attention to the movie.

Mel appears to do the same. She tries to relax and curls up in her corner of the couch to watch the movie, too. The sad part about relaxing lately is that when I relax, I get sleepy. With my mind clear, body relaxes and the warmth cause my eyelids to begin to close.

I don't think I fell asleep, but I must've. The next thing I know something yanks me off the couch. My eyes open wide to see who does the pulling on me and I start to struggle. "No, no, no..." Mike twists me into his arms, my back to his front. An arm snakes around my waist and a large knife suddenly presses to my throat. The door to the apartment slams open and feet begin to stomp up the stairs. Mike's able to get ahold of me. He went undetected until it was too late. I'm going to die.

Mel screams. I don't know what she says. Mike yells at her as men barge into the room. So much commotion and confusion starts. There're the screams from Mel, demands and yells from the men and then there's Mike. His grip on me is tight and I can feel the blade of the knife on my throat. I know if I move it'll be for the last time. I swallow deep and can feel the blade bite into my skin just when I do that.

A sudden growl erupts in the room. "Enough!" I hear Gabe shout loudly over everyone. Then there's silence. Mel runs over to Jack and he takes her into his arms where she cries. Gordon steps in front of her to shield her view of me and sets his hand on his gun. My stomach tightens at this thought.

"Mike, please let the girl go," Gordon asks with a firm, but calm voice.

Mike stands a little taller and shifts me farther in front of him to shield his body. "The bitch needs to die." He sneers.

The words that drip from Mike's lips send a shiver up my spine. This is it. He has me right where he wants me.

Gabe raises his hands in surrender and takes a step forward. "Man, please. If you let her go we can work something out." He speaks like he means business—so serious.

"Don't come any fucking closer or I'll cut her!" Mike sneers his evil words as he pushes the blade tighter to my throat. I whine in pain as the blade breaks skin and a little blood drips down my neck.

Gabe stops his move with his hands still in the air. "She's not your problem, man. Just let her go." Gabe's voice is a little on the demanding side. If I notice this, then I'm sure Mike does, too.

"Back the fuck off, man. I'm not kidding," Mike growls this time.

Gabe steps back. "Okay, okay. Can we talk about it?"

I begin to feel overwhelmed. My emotions swamp me—the fear, the anger, it's an overload that drains me. I feel weak and I'm tired of the idle chit chat. "Mike, please let me go," I whisper so the blade held on my throat doesn't dig in any more than it already has.

"Shut up, bitch!" Mike grinds his pelvis into my backside. "You feel that? Yeah, you loved that when you had it. Had to go fuck it up and send me to prison. Stupid bitch. Now you will get what's coming to you."

Everything moves in slow motion after that. The blade moves from my neck while Mike is distracted. Jack appears to be sneaking up from the side. How I didn't see that happening, I don't know. The knife moves enough where I can look from Jack over to Gabe, who suddenly moves in my direction. Gordon has his gun at hand and then there's pain. It's all pain. Mike sinks the sharp blade into my side just seconds before a gunshot rings across the room.

Mike's grip on me is gone. The pain consumes me and down I go to the floor. I don't think I've ever felt such pain before in my life. Even when Mike and his buddies did those unthinkable things to me, that pain doesn't compare.

I hold my side and look to Mike. Is he dead? He isn't moving, but I don't know if he's dead. Suddenly, Gabe's at my side. My vision gets blurry and my head feels fuzzy. The room spins. I only have one final thought. "I love you, Gabe." And everything goes black.

CHAPTER 25

Belle

I wake to voices all around me. I can't seem to open my eyes yet, but I know in time I will.

"He won't be getting out for a very long time."

"He missed every major artery, so we just have to wait for her to wake up. I'm just glad there were no problems with the anesthetic this time."

Gabe. He's talking to someone, explaining something or telling those bits and pieces, details of the case. I'm not sure. I'm having trouble waking completely. I lay and wait for the fog to lift, just listening. More familiar voices enter the room. Mel's here and there's Jack. Everyone's safe. Thank God.

I feel someone move some hair from my forehead. "Belle. You going to wake up for us?" Gabe asks. I'd know that voice anywhere. I try to open my eyes. My eyelids feel heavy, but I manage to get them open. The first sight I see is a smiling Gabe looking down on me. "There she is." He leans down and kisses my forehead.

"Hi," I whisper. It seems to be the only form of speaking I've been doing lately and my throat's sore at the moment. I need to know what's going on, so I look around the room. The gang is all here. Jack, Mel and Gabe.

"You are okay, Belle. You are safe. We're all safe now." Gabe smiles.

"What happened?" I ask him.

Gabe sits down in the chair beside the bed and takes my hand in his. "We don't know how he did it, but he managed to slip in unseen. We had every angle covered so we don't understand." He sighs.

"I have a technician checking the cameras to see what the problem was, to see why they didn't detect him. I feel like this is my fault. I'm sorry, Belle," Jack says. Mel wraps her arms around his shoulders in support.

"Don't blame yourself, Jack." My voice gets stronger. I lick my lips and try to moisten the utter dryness. "Deep down I knew he'd get to me regardless." I look at Jack and Mel. I don't want any of them to blame themselves for Mike's actions. He's the one to blame, no one else.

Jack shrugs. "I'm just glad you are okay."

"Thank you," I tell him. "What about Mike?" I ask them all. "Is he dead?"

The room gets quiet. I wait as I look from one to the other. No one seems to want to answer. I glare at Gabe.

"No. He is alive, but he's hurting. Once he's out of the hospital he'll be put in prison for a very long time." He takes a breath. "He won't be hurting you anymore, Belle. You don't have to go to any court proceedings or anything."

Well, this is somewhat reassuring. I wish Mike was dead, but locked up will have to do. Now the big question is how the fuck did he get in the apartment?

I try to adjust myself in the bed because I want to sit up, but it hurts to do. I wince. Gabe stops me. "Belle. Use the damn controls. Don't hurt yourself, woman!" he grunts.

There's my man. Even with me being in the hospital, my man will put me in my place no matter how sick I am. I reach over to the controls and raise the head of the bed to my comfort. My mouth feels real dry and in need of something to drink.

"Drink?" I ask. Instantly Mel is up. She grabs the cup of ice water off the table and hands it to me. I take a few little sips to wet my mouth. Damn, that feels better. I hand the cup back and she sits down. "How did Mike get in the apartment?" I look to Gabe, who then puts his hand on the back of his neck and squeezes. His expression becomes angry and then he looks like he wants to cry. Seriously, my man looks vulnerable.

"Apparently there is an escape hatch on the roof that opens into an attic to the apartment." He blows out a breath. "I honestly didn't know about it and feel completely stupid for not knowing. If I had known, I could've probably stopped him." Gabe leans back in his chair, eyes shut tight. I can tell he is beating himself up over it.

"Gabe, there was nothing you could've done differently. Why can't any of you understand that? Mike outsmarted us. Plain and simple. He had years of plotting. I was just the unwilling victim. But now it's over. We all need to move on." I look to each of them. I try to speak to them with my eyes, to prove to them that I mean what I say. We're not getting any younger, and I have now survived that bastard twice and have been lucky enough to survive cancer. It's time to move forward, time to look to the future.

Mel and Jack leave after our chat. The doctor comes in and explains my injury. Then the doctor tells me that I can go home tomorrow. Apparently, I'd been sleeping for two days post anesthetic, but they were monitoring me closely.

Speaking of going home—I don't have a home anymore. I think I should bring this up with Gabe. I'm not sure if living with him is something permanent that he wants, even though I know I do. I clear my throat to get his attention. He seems to stare into space thinking about something. "Gabe?"

He looks over to me and slowly smiles. "Yes, my sweet girl?"

I bite my lip because I'm not really sure how to ask. "So...I—uh..." I blow out my breath. "I need a place to stay. I know I've been staying with you and now, since that jackass burned my place down, I really need a place." I sigh. "So..." I begin to fidget with my fingers.

A smirk rises on Gabe's mouth. "Are you asking to move in with me, Belle?" The smirk is full force now.

I want to reach over to him and smack him. I know he's just teasing me now, but still. I can feel myself blush. My shy side is coming out. This man can bring all sides out of me. "You jerk!" I mumble.

Gabe wiggles his eyebrows at me. "Well, are you?"

I can't help but giggle at his persistent teasing. "Yes. Now are you having fun teasing me? You big goof!" I laugh.

Gabe chuckles before he smiles. "It'd be my pleasure to have you live with me." The smile fades and he becomes serious. "I love you, Belle. I'll love you until the end of time. What's mine is yours, so if you need a home, my home is yours."

Gabe's words touch me deeply. I want to cry because I'm so happy. "Thank you for loving me. I love you so much."

EPILOGUE

Belle

It's Tuesday afternoon and it's been three weeks since everything went down with Mike. My wound has healed nicely and I feel good. Gabe has opened the bar again and business is good. Jack has decided he wants to stick around the area—I think he and Mel are hitting it off.

I returned to work last week on a part-time basis. I just want to ease back into things. Mel took today off so we could go shopping and catch a movie. She's been working lots trying to distract her mind from that night and the after effects and such by keeping busy. My girl is strong, but I know even strong girls break eventually, so shopping and a movie it is.

"How are things with you and Gabe?" Mel asks me.

I browse the rack of clothing and think over the past few weeks. I smile to myself. "Things have been great." I think about the handcuffs, the sex toys and Gabe's husky voice while we play. A tingly feeling comes over me. I shouldn't be thinking of these things in public.

"Well, that's good. I'm so happy for you both. You deserve to be happy," Mel says as she too searches through the rack for something that might interest her. She pulls a shirt from the rack and lifts it up to show me. "What about this?" She holds up a purple silky shirt, tank style. It's nice.

"Hmm, not bad," I tell her.

My cell phone goes off in my purse. I dig into my bag and pull it out.

I look at the screen and confusion sets in. I look at Mel. "Hey, does this mean anything to you?" I show her my phone.

Mel's body freezes. She is stunned into silence. I wave my other hand in front of her face to get her attention. After a few moments Mel finally blinks and looks up to me.

"Belle remember when I said I needed to talk to you about something?"

Message: The boys are back in town.

Stay tuned for more of Belle and Gabe in Mel and Jack's book. Losing Control: Circumstances #2

ABOUT THE AUTHOR

Jean is just a small town girl looking for a little adventure. With her love of reading and writing she wanted to explore and see what her characters could do for her. Being a full time nurse, a wife, and mother of two boys, she has her hands full, but takes the time to dream among the pages. She is a true blooded Canadian and hopes to explore parts of the world sometime in the future, but for now, she explores in the books she reads and writes. Being a huge Indie Author fan, she has made several friends online and has met a few at book signings. Hoping to one day meet some fans face to face, she would gladly friend you on Facebook, Goodreads, and Google+.

She can be found on Facebook:
https://www.facebook.com/jean.kelso.14
She can be found on Goodreads:
https://www.goodreads.com/author/show/8338589.Jean_Kelso
She can be found on Google+ as Barb Jean Kelso Johnson